'You've heard about my climbing accident?'

'Yes.' She cleared her throat nervously. 'It was in the Press.'

'I threw that to the gossip columns so I could keep the really juicy titbit secret for as long as possible.' The grooves either side of Bran's mouth deepened. 'I fancy you know what I'm going to say. My stupid accident, on a climb I've made dozens of times before, has left me with a somewhat inconvenient legacy for an artist. In short, I'm blind.'

Dear Reader

Helo and *Croeso-i-Gymru* — Welcome to Wales! Yes, this month we are inviting you to this beautiful country which, as you will discover, should not be underestimated as a destination for a scintillating love-affair! Indeed, Catherine George's Euromance reveals the true character and appeal of the Welsh culture and scenery — so sit back and revel in this unique setting for a romance that will take your breath away. . . *Hwyl Fawr*!

The Editor

The author says:

'Married, with two children, I was born in a Welsh mining village, where from childhood I was filled with the national love of music, preferably operatic, and of rugby. We have lived in Brazil and in various parts of the British Isles before settling in our present home overlooking the picturesque River Wye. In LAIR OF THE DRAGON I have used the area for which I feel the deepest affinity: the incomparably beautiful Welsh Borders.'

Catherine George

★ TURN TO THE BACK PAGES OF THIS BOOK FOR *WELCOME TO EUROPE*. . .OUR FASCINATING FACT-FILE ★

LAIR OF THE DRAGON

BY

CATHERINE GEORGE

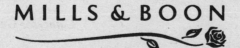

MILLS & BOON LIMITED
ETON HOUSE, 18–24 PARADISE ROAD
RICHMOND, SURREY, TW9 1SR

First published in Great Britain 1994
by Mills & Boon Limited

© Catherine George 1994

Australian copyright 1994
Philippine copyright 1994
This edition 1994

ISBN 0 263 78418 5

Set in 10 on 11 pt Linotron Times
01-9403-52210

Typeset in Great Britain by Centracet, Cambridge
Made and printed in Great Britain

CHAPTER ONE

THE crowded sales-room was so hot that Naomi yearned to leave once her part in the bidding was over. A ninety-piece ironstone dinner service was waiting for her to collect afterwards, along with a Minton dessert set and a pair of Chamberlain's Worcester vases, all the pieces acquired at a price which would delight her London employer. For this was Cardiff, where the truly phenomenal sums were reserved for Swansea and Nantgarw porcelain, and London buyers rarely competed against their Welsh colleagues. An almost cathedral-like hush had filled the sales-room as the bidding rose to its climax on the few such items on sale.

Up to now Naomi's interest had been professional and automatic as she noted prices alongside every lot, whether instructed to bid or not. As usual she'd taken pains to look inconspicuous, her jeans and jersey giving no hint of the large sums at her disposal. But now her bidding role was over and the part she'd been dreading was at hand. The auctioneer cast a bland smile over the assembly and announced a list of small individual items, starting with a Derby piece depicting two dancing figures. Naomi shot another apprehensive look round the crowded room, but the face she was searching for was still nowhere in sight. And if it had been she'd have known. She'd set eyes on Bran Llewellyn only once, but the experience had been more than enough to imprint his face on her memory for all time.

A month previously she had been sent to a similar

sale here in Cardiff. To her chagrin she'd been outbidden on every item her employer wanted, then afterwards the car had refused to start for the journey back to London. Naomi had found a garage to deal with the car by next day, rang her employer to tell him what was happening, then on Rupert Sinclair's advice took a room at the Park Hotel, a mere stone's throw from the New Theatre. All the irritations of the day were forgotten when she discovered the Welsh National Opera were giving a performance of *La Bohème* that very night. Naomi had ignored the 'sold out' signs and hurried to enquire for any returns. To her delight she'd been offered a seat in the circle, and she had gone off to the theatre very happily later, feeling like a child given an unexpected treat as she mounted the cream and gilt stairs from the theatre foyer to the attractive, serpentine circle bar. Glad she'd worn a suit for once, she had threaded through the crowd on her way to find her excellent second-row seat in the circle, then studied her programme as the orchestra tuned up, impressed to learn that the production was a new one by a rising young director, with sets designed by the celebrated Welsh artist, Bran Llewellyn.

A sharp tingle of anticipation had shot through Naomi as the curtain rose at the end of the overture to tumultous applause for the famous garret studio setting. The artist had stamped the scene with his own individual style and panache, even to providing the portrait Marcello, the baritone, was painting of the pretty, half-nude model, who was the only one on stage to stay mute as the opera began. All the frustrations of the day had melted away as Naomi lost herself in the music, and when the exquisite duet between Mimi and Rudolfo brought the house down at the end of the first act she'd made her way to the bar in a dream, with the melody still ringing in her head. Drinks were waiting on the numbered ledge all round the bar for those who'd ordered earlier, but Naomi had joined the throng for coffee, where disaster suddenly struck. As she turned away from the bar with her cup a tall, dark man in a dinner-jacket cannoned into her, almost knocking her over.

By some miracle of self-preservation Naomi had somehow managed to retain her balance and the coffee as the man grabbed her by the elbows, his handsome face aghast. He apologised profusely in a deep, musical, voice, offered to buy her another coffee, a drink, anything to make amends, but Naomi, scarlet and mute, had shaken her head to everything, and made her escape as fast as she could, overwhelmed by the fact that from the photograph in her programme her charismatic assailant was none other than Bran Llewellyn himself.

Naomi came to with a start as she realised the auctioneer was halfway through the list of miscellaneous items, her heart giving a great thump as she heard him announce a particularly fine piece of Leeds creamware.

'A subtle piece for the discerning taste,' said the auctioneer invitingly, and went on to extol the beauty of the clear rich tint of the creamware chestnut tureen, a lidded vessel perforated by hand in the late eighteenth century, with double twisted handles ending in flowers and foliage of exquisite subtlety.

This time Naomi deliberately turned round in her seat, craning her neck in all directions, but there was no sign of the unmistakable, flamboyant figure her sister had been so sure would be present. Unless Bran Llewellyn was disguised as an umbrella stand he hadn't turned up after all. Passionately grateful to him for his absence, Naomi relaxed and concentrated on the bidding, which was fast and furious, culminating in the sale of the tureen for an astronomical sum to a telephone bidder.

Since this was the only piece likely to have lured the famous artist to the sale, a great load rolled off Naomi's shoulders. The prospect of trying to ingratiate herself with the man on her sister's behalf had been hanging over her like the sword of Damocles.

Afterwards, after writing a large company cheque in the office, Naomi began on the endless task of wrapping every last individual dish of the services she'd acquired. When one of the porters, sympathetic with the small, toiling figure, offered to help her downstairs with the boxes, Naomi thanked him fervently, and after a minute or two managed to steer the conversation to the Leeds tureen.

'I was hoping to nab that,' she said untruthfully, swathing a Worcester vase in bubble-wrap. 'It went overseas, I suppose.'

The man shook his head, leaning close. 'Not supposed to say, mind, but just for the record it stays in Wales — went to Bran Llewellyn, the artist.'

Naomi's hands stilled. 'Really?'

The porter nodded importantly. 'He collects the stuff. Look,' he added, 'if you're parked in the multistorey, nip out and get your car. Bring it to the door and I'll carry these boxes down for you. Too heavy for a little thing like you.'

Naomi did as he said with alacrity, and a few minutes later managed to find a parking space directly outside the building. When her genial helper had finished stowing the boxes in the back for her she smiled at him gratefully. 'How kind you are. Thank you so much. By the way,' she added casually, 'I'm disappointed Bran Llewellyn didn't turn up in person. I was hoping to get his autograph.'

He nodded. 'He usually does. But he had an accident last week, climbing on the Carmarthen Vans. I know a chap who delivers oil to his place up near Llanthony——' The porter stopped suddenly and shut the boot with a bang. 'I shouldn't be telling you this, love. Good thing you're not a reporter!'

Naomi winced. 'I won't say a word,' she assured him, and got in the car. She wound down the window. 'If he's an artist I hope the poor man didn't injure his hands.'

'That's a fact!' The man retreated quickly as one of his colleagues emerged from the building. 'Safe journey, then.'

Naomi, never the world's most courageous driver, was obliged to keep her mind firmly on what she was doing as she found her way out of Cardiff and back to the M4, with no thought to spare for Bran Llewellyn until she was chugging along in the slow lane on her way towards the Severn Bridge and London.

How on earth had her sister slipped up about the artist's accident? thought Naomi, baffled. Admittedly Diana worked in the features department of the *Chronicle*; nevertheless she rarely missed any hard news that came in. Naomi frowned, hoping the artist had suffered nothing too terrible in the way of injuries. At the same time she was deeply thankful he'd been prevented from attending the sale. After hearing about the incident at the theatre, Diana had been obsessed with the idea of an article about him. Her master plan had been for Naomi to buttonhole Bran Llewellyn at the sale, remind him about their accidental meeting, then persuade him to give an interview to her sister. The prospect had given Naomi nightmares. She not only quailed at the prospect of pushing herself at Bran Llewellyn, but knew only too well that he was famous for his scathing opinion of the Press, who tended to give him a hard time in the gossip columns.

Nevertheless, since bumping into Bran Llewellyn at the opera, Naomi was secretly as obsessed by him as Diana and had done a little private research of her own. She'd learned that he was hailed by some as the greatest Welsh artist since Augustus John, and was successful enough to be notoriously choosy about the commissions he accepted. He was skilled at both landscapes and portraits, and the latter were commissions he accepted these days only when the sitter's looks touched some chord in him. Consequently his studies of gnarled age were renowned, and lately even the simplest of his drawings fetched impressive prices. As if his formidable talent weren't enough, the Welsh artist possessed romantically wild good looks and a personality larger than life, with a charisma that drew women like bees to a honeypot, though to date he remained unmarried. And while women kept throwing themselves at him he'd probably stay that way, thought Naomi, annoyed with herself for a pang of illogical jealousy.

It was late in the evening by the time Naomi arrived in Kensington to report on the success of her day. Rupert Sinclair, fiftyish, sophisticated, lazy, and a highly respected authority in the field of ceramics, was waiting for her. Naomi had learnt a great deal from him since joining Sinclair Antiques. In return she'd gradually taken over the firm's bookkeeping from Rupert, who hated figures as much as Naomi liked them.

'What a clever girl,' he drawled, inspecting the contents of the boxes. 'Did you pack this lot yourself?'

'Who else?' said Naomi tartly. 'Though a nice Welsh porter did help me carry the stuff down to the car.'

Rupert, anxious to join his wife for dinner in the flat

above, patted Naomi's dark head. 'Take a taxi home, darling, you deserve it.'

The telephone was ringing as Naomi let herself into the poky flat she shared with a friend. Clare was away on holiday, which meant there was no meal waiting and the place felt very empty. Naomi sighed wearily as she picked up the receiver.

'Naomi?'

'Hello, Di.'

'You don't have to tell me. I know you didn't see him. The wretched man's had an accident, so it was a bit of a wild-goose chase for you after all——'

'It was nothing of the kind. I went to Cardiff to bid at the auction for Rupert, remember.'

Diana, a very single-minded lady when it came to her job, brushed that aside. 'Never mind Rupert. You'll never guess what I found out about our artist today! Crispin says Bran Llewellyn's been commissioned to write his autobiography.'

'And Crispin Dacre's never wrong!'

'As well as being my dear, faithful friend, Crispin's the best gossip columnist in the business; never misses a trick. He says Diadem's persuaded our artist to write his life story—bound to make number one first week on the list. Crispin was in school with one of the Diadem senior editors, so he was first to know our charismatic Celt had agreed.'

'Spiffing,' said Naomi, yawning. 'Now if you don't mind I'm off to take a shower, go to bed, and dream of doing nothing at all for three whole weeks. My holiday can't come soon enough.'

'I was just coming to that,' said Diana, something in her voice turning Naomi's blood cold. 'Listen, love, how about doing me the most wonderful favour?'

Before her conversation with Diana Naomi had been dog-tired. Afterwards she was so uptight that it took her until three in the morning to fall into a restless doze, haunted by dreams of a menacing figure which pursued her relentlessly, brandishing a giant paintbrush.

Diana Barry had joined the *Chronicle* straight from university, armed with an English degree and a personality like a Centurion tank. Now, several years on, she was a respected sub-editor on Features, her only weakness a consuming passion for Craig Anthony, the features editor. Diana had chestnut hair, flashing dark eyes, a tall, generously curved figure and lived in a constant state of frustration because Craig seemed immune to her charms. Her constant aim was some way to show him she was not only desirable, clever, and a good journalist, but the perfect soul-mate to share his life.

'All I need,' she had told Naomi, time and time again, 'is to bring off some *coup* big enough to peel the scales from his gorgeous blue eyes.'

And at last Diana felt she'd hit on the exact thing. Only she needed her sister's help to bring it off.

'Are you mad?' Naomi howled down the phone. 'I won't do it.'

Diana was undeterred, even when Naomi slammed down the phone. She promptly took a taxi round to the flat, installed herself in the one comfortable armchair and talked at her sister until Naomi was at screaming point.

The plan, in theory, was simple. Via Crispin Dacre Diana had learned that the famous Welsh artist would have no truck with a biographer. He would write his own life story or Diadem could push off.

'Only I don't suppose he said "push" off!'

Naomi glared at her sister. 'I don't care what he said. I'm not *doing* it.'

Diadem, went on Diana, unmoved, were providing

Bran Llewellyn with a secretary to work on the book with him in Wales for a couple of weeks, and Crispin had persuaded his editor chum to give Diana the job. The artist, it seemed, could spare only a short time for the project, the end product of which was to be a glossy affair, with coloured plates of the artist's work and the biographical details kept to a minimum.

'It's so maddening!' said Diana, jumping up to pace up and down. 'Just think of the article I could write if I actually stayed in the man's house, but Naomi, I *can't*.'

'Why not?'

'I've had every scrap of leave coming to me, but apart from that I daren't take off from the *Chronicle* at the moment because Craig's deputy is leaving to work on the *Financial Times*, and I stand a fair chance of getting his job. If I pulled this article off I'd definitely get it.' She pulled a face. 'In any case Bran Llewellyn's notorious for being able to smell a journalist a mile off.' She turned to Naomi with a cajoling smile. 'While you, my pet, are very obviously nothing to do with the Press, type very efficiently, and, best of all, have three weeks' holiday coming to you.'

'Which I do *not* intend to spend working like a dog in the Black Mountains of Gwent,' snapped Naomi.

'How do you know where he lives?' pounced Diana.

'The porter from the auction house told me. Not that it matters where the man lives. I'm not going near the place.'

Diana fixed her with pleading brown eyes. 'Not even to help me gain my heart's desire?'

'Don't talk such tosh!'

'It's true. If I scoop an interview with Bran Llewellyn I just know Craig will——'

'What do you mean, *you* scoop an interview?' demanded Naomi hotly. 'I'd be doing that, if you have your way—which you're not. I'm going home to the bosom of our family for a week's spoiling, and then I'm going on a nice little drive around the Lake District in the fresh air, all by myself. . .' She trailed into silence. 'Why are you looking at me like that?' she asked suspiciously.

'I hate having to resort to this,' said Diana miserably. 'But think back to the time when Greg walked out on you. Who picked up the pieces and put you back together again?'

'You did,' muttered Naomi, deflating like a pricked balloon.

'Exactly. And I was happy to do it, because you needed me.' Diana's eyes filled with entreaty. 'Well now, little sister, I need you. I know it smacks of emotional blackmail, but say you'll do it for me, Naomi. *Please*! It's only for a couple of weeks. My happiness—my whole future could depend on it.'

Naomi stared at her sister despairingly. 'I wish I'd never told you about bumping into Bran Llewellyn that night in Cardiff. You've been obsessed with the idea of an exclusive on him ever since.' She groaned, turning away from the pleading in Diana's eyes. 'Yes—of course I'll do it. If it means so much to you, what choice do I have?'

Diana threw her arms round Naomi and hugged the life out of her. 'You angel—I knew you wouldn't let me down. Now all you have to do is record brief details of your c.v. on tape and send it off to Diadem. Miles Hay—Crispin's chum—will forward it to Bran Llewellyn.'

'A *tape*?' exploded Naomi, pulling free. 'Are you kidding?'

Diana shrugged. 'Not my fault if the wretched man is cranky. Apparently our artist has a thing about voices—probably because he's Welsh. He prefers a tape to a letter of application. Don't scowl like that,' she added, sighing, then gave Naomi a look straight from the heart. 'I've never asked your help before, love.'

Which was such an incontrovertible truth that Naomi made the recording next day, feeling utterly ridiculous, then sent it off to Miles Hay, certain Bran Llewellyn would take an instant dislike to her voice. But only three days later the editor wrote that Mr Llewellyn was pleased to confirm the temporary secretarial post, and mentioned a fixed sum which took her breath away. Would she please report to Gwal-y-Ddraig by the following Wednesday at the latest?

'Bran Llewellyn must have liked my voice,' she told Diana tersely on the phone.

There was silence on the line for a moment. 'It's fate,' said her sister, sounding awed. 'Naomi, I'll never forget this.'

'I don't suppose I shall either,' retorted Naomi. 'My one consolation is the money I'm getting, which is quite fantastic compared with the peanuts Rupert pays me.' Her voice softened with affection. 'Besides, *you* were there for *me* when I needed you, heaven knows. But you owe me a holiday for this.'

'If this comes off I'll stand you a fortnight in the Bahamas,' promised Diana rashly, '*and* bully Rupert into giving you the time off.'

'After a spell in the lair of the dragon I'm likely to need it!'

'*Where*?'

'Home of Bran Llewellyn. I looked it up. That's the name of his house—Gwal-y-Ddraig, lair of the dragon.'

'I don't like the sound of that. As soon as you get there, give me the phone number,' ordered Diana, sounding alarmed. 'And make sure you keep the man at arm's length.'

'Don't be silly!' said Naomi, laughing. 'He probably won't even notice I'm there.'

'Now you're being silly. I wonder if he'll remember you?'

'I very much doubt it. By the way, does Craig know I'm going there?'

'Absolutely not! Have *you* told anyone?'

'No fear. Rupert would probably sack me on the spot. And everyone else of my acquaintance would think I'm mad.'

Naomi was tense with nerves by the end of her car journey from London, though the drive down the motorway had been pleasant enough in the spring sunshine. After crossing the Severn Bridge the journey was swift and uneventful along dual carriageways and major roads which took her past Abergavenny on the road for Hereford for a few miles until she reached the signpost—so suddenly she almost missed the turn— for Llanfihangel Crucorney. And suddenly, with no transition, Naomi found herself transported back in time, as by the simple expedient of leaving a modern highway she found herself deep in the Welsh Marches. Unspoilt and ravishingly beautiful in the spring sunlight as the area was, the blood-soaked drama of its past was hard to believe as the quiet road wound towards the next landmark on her route, the Skirrid Inn, the oldest public house in the Principality of Wales.

Naomi suddenly yearned for tea, or lemonade, or anything to quench a thirst which was sudden and overwhelming. But, recognising the longing as a sub-conscious attempt to postpone the meeting with Bran Llewellyn, she passed the inn and turned left again at

a signpost for Cwmyoy and Llanthony, down a narrow
steep road which levelled out after a short distance to
meander on its convoluted way through the Vale of
Ewyas.

It was impossible to drive at any speed, since the
twisting, turning road was narrow, with passing places
for cars to edge past each other when absolutely
necessary. Much to Naomi's relief she met virtually no
traffic, and despite her mounting tension was able to
enjoy the beautiful scenery at leisure as she drove
along a road edged by low, barbered hedges. Because
her previous visits to Wales had been restricted to
Cardiff and the windswept beaches of Pembrokeshire,
she had visualised the Black Mountains as a bleak,
austere place, inhospitable and hostile to intruders
from beyond Offa's Dyke.

Nothing could have been further from the truth.
Instead of great barren jagged peaks the mountains
were sensuously rounded, as though a mythical race of
giants had built a series of burial mounds for their
kings along the bed of the Honddu, the small river
which splashed companionably below, dictating the
serpentine meanderings of the road.

The mountains, far from being black or bleak, wore
bronze crowns of bracken above purple cloaks slashed
with bright green, where decidous trees not yet in leaf
grew cheek-by-jowl with feathery young conifers. And
below the mantle of planted trees lay gentler slopes
which bordered the road in a colourful patchwork of
small, sheep-dotted fields edged by tidy hedgerows
starred with daffodils.

The noise, to Naomi's delight and amusement, was
quite extraordinary. She rolled down the window,
amazed by the sheer volume of sound as she passed
lambing sheds at the farms en route. The air, warm
and spring-scented, fairly vibrated with the ovine

chorus as she pulled over into one of the wider passing places to study the directions for the last lap of her journey.

Gwal-y-Ddraig, when she finally managed to find it, lay at the end of a steep drive which wound up through a forest of conifers to nowhere until the house swam into view like a mirage in an oasis of gardens backed by the mountain slope. Solid and four-square, built of rose-bronze sandstone, Bran Llewellyn's house came as a surprise. For one thing it was much smaller and less grand than she'd expected, with small, multi-paned windows and a plain oak door. But as Naomi got out of the car she could see another large building at the back, joined to the main house by a stone passageway. And, as confirmation that she'd found the right house, a weathervane on the roof flaunted a gleaming brass replica of the dragon on the Welsh national flag.

Suffering a bad attack of cold feet at the sight of Bran Llewellyn's home, Naomi stiffened her back-bone, reminding herself that the money was fabulous and, whatever happened, the time would soon pass. She lifted her suitcases from the car and put them down in front of the main door, then rang the old-fashioned iron bell.

After a short interval the door opened wide to reveal, not the great artist himself, to Naomi's relief, but a thin, friendly woman in a neat navy dress. She beamed as she stretched out a hand in greeting.

'Welcome to Gwal-y-Ddraig. You'll be Miss Barry. Come in, come in, you must be tired after driving so far. London, isn't it? Follow me and I'll take you straight up to your room, then you can come down and meet Bran. He's in his studio at the moment, but while you tidy up I'll tell him you're here and he'll see you in the garden-room——' She stopped suddenly.

'There's silly of me, I forgot to say who I am. Megan Griffiths, housekeeper.'

'How do you do?' said Naomi, much cheered by the warmth of her welcome as she followed the bustling figure up the stairs leading from the small, square hall.

Megan opened a door on the landing and ushered Naomi into a sunny bedroom with a tester bed and flower-sprigged curtains at windows which gave breathtaking views of the garden and the valley below.

'I hope you'll be comfortable.' She opened another door. 'Here's your own bathroom, and there's a tray with kettle and china on the chest. You can help yourself to a cup of tea whenever you fancy one.'

'You're very kind. It's a charming room, Mrs Griffiths.' Naomi smiled warmly.

'Megan, please. And Tal will fetch your things. Tal's my husband,' Megan explained.

'Thank you. If you give me a minute or two to tidy up I'll be ready to meet Mr Llewellyn.' Naomi quailed inwardly at the prospect. 'Shall I find my own way to the garden-room?'

'Yes, if you like. It's to the right of the front door.'

No point in putting off the evil hour, thought Naomi when she was alone. In the small, beautifully appointed bathroom she washed her face, tidied her hair, then carefully applied a touch of discreet war-paint before setting out to confront the master of Gwal-y-Ddraig.

Naomi walked slowly down the stairs, running her hand over the carved wood banister, then halted halfway down, her attention caught by the dramatic landscape on the wall below. Even without the 'LL' of the initial in the corner it was instantly recognisable as the artist's work. Naomi gazed at it with a shiver, suddenly conscious of the enormity of what she was doing as she went down the remaining stairs to tap on the door of the garden-room.

When a deep, peremptory voice called, 'Come,' Naomi opened the door on a low-ceilinged, uncluttered room which seemed to merit its name solely because the French windows in one wall opened out into the garden. Late sunshine streamed into the room casting yellow fingers of light over the carpet towards the feet of the man standing very still by the fireplace.

Naomi's previous glimpse of Bran Llewellyn had been brief in the extreme, allowing little time for details. Now she could see he was tall for a Welshman, and powerfully built. He stood with hands thrust in pockets, his head thrown back, the familiar shock of coal-black hair longer than when she'd seen him last. He wore a dark green sweatshirt tucked into khaki trousers, espadrilles on his bare brown feet. And now she was actually in his presence again she realised that the face she found so hard to forget was arresting rather than conventionally handsome. His forehead was domed and leonine and his eyebrows arched thick above heavy-lidded eyes set well apart above a long, prominent nose, but the face was expressionless other than a hint of the sensual in the curve of his wide, tightly closed mouth. As Naomi approached him she saw that stitches had recently been removed from one cheek, leaving a red scar.

She cleared her throat nervously, holding out her hand. 'Good evening. I'm Naomi Barry.'

'Welcome to Gwal-y-Ddraig,' he answered, ignoring the hand.

Naomi let it fall, mortified because in her heart of hearts she'd hoped he'd remember her. 'Thank you.'

Bran Llewellyn sat down in one of the tall-backed chairs flanking the fireplace, waving her towards the other. 'Tell me about yourself.'

'What would you like to know, Mr Llewellyn?'

'Begin at the beginning.'

'But I sent the tape you asked for——'

'Obviously,' he interrupted. 'Nevertheless, now you're here in person please be good enough to refresh my memory.'

Naomi forced herself to speak calmly as she told the still, attentive man that she'd been born in Cheltenham, received the usual secondary education and gone on to take an English degree at London University, and then a job as a business researcher with a management consultancy before her present employment.

'What made you change to work in a shop?' he asked.

She stiffened. 'Because I find the work interesting. I'm quite good with figures, I can type, and I enjoy dealing with the public, all necessary requirements for someone working at Sinclair Antiques. I occasionally attend sales at places like Sotheby's, something I find stimulating——' She stopped, her attention caught suddenly by the alcove at the far end of the room, where a familiar chestnut tureen formed a centrepiece to a magnificent display of porcelain and pottery.

'What is it?' the deep voice enquired.

'I was looking at your collection of porcelain— especially the Leeds creamware.' Naomi turned to him with a polite little smile.

'It's not to everyone's taste.'

'I can't imagine why it's not. Personally I adore that deep creamy tint——' She broke off, flushing. 'Sorry.'

'Don't apologise for enthusiasm!' His mouth turned down at the corners. 'If you must know, it was your experience with ceramics which influenced me to take you on. That, and the way you speak. My main requirement was a pleasing voice.' He shrugged. 'I felt

I could live with yours for however long it takes to commit my life to paper.'

'I hope it's no longer than three weeks, Mr Llewellyn,' she said at once.

'Why?'

'Because that's exactly how much leave I've got coming to me from my job. I made that clear on the tape. I was told you were in a hurry to complete the work in that time, otherwise I wouldn't have applied.'

'I'm aware of that,' he said impatiently. 'I've dictated most of it already, so if there's any hold-up it'll be on your part, not mine.'

Naomi tried not to bristle. 'There's no danger of that, Mr Llewellyn——'

'Good. A rough first draft is all that's necessary. One of the editors from Diadem will take over from there.'

'Then perhaps you'd tell me what routine you require, Mr Llewellyn——'

'My first requirement is use of first names,' he said sardonically. 'For both of us.'

Naomi inclined her head. 'Whatever you say. No doubt you'll want to read through my day's work each evening before——'

'No!' he said, with such force that she blinked, taken aback.

'I—I'm sorry?'

'Let me put you right about this "routine" of yours,' he went on. 'You start at nine each morning, with a suitable break for coffee, lunch and so on, and carry on working until five in the afternoon.'

'Of course. But I don't mind working longer hours than that if it means getting the job down, Mr—Bran.'

'Not *Mr*, just plain Bran.' His mouth curved in a cold, mirthless smile. 'And don't worry, Naomi Barry. You'll earn your money. You'll have homework to do every evening—which is where the pleasant voice bit comes in. You'll be obliged to read back the day's work to me every night after dinner.'

Naomi sat very still, cold with the sudden realisation that the eyes beneath Bran Llewellyn's lowered lids had never looked directly into hers from the moment she'd walked into the room. She swallowed, seized with a sharp pang of prescience.

'I sense by the pregnant pause that you've worked out the reason,' he said harshly. 'You've heard about my climbing accident?'

'Yes.' She cleared her throat nervously. 'It was in the Press.'

'I threw that to the gossip columns so I could keep the really juicy titbit secret for as long as possible.' The grooves either side of his mouth deepened. 'I fancy you know what I'm going to say. My bloody stupid accident, on a climb I've made dozens of times before, has left me with a somewhat inconvenient legacy for an artist. In short, I'm blind.'

CHAPTER TWO

NAOMI gazed in horror at the bitter, morose face, totally at a loss for something to say.

'Well?' he demanded irritably. 'Cat got your tongue? Surely you've got some comment to make.' He scowled. 'Don't tell me you're a sniveller!'

'Certainly not,' she said, stung into response. 'The news came as a shock, that's all. I had no idea——'

'Bloody good thing, too,' he snapped. 'It's not something I want broadcast, so keep it to yourself, please.'

'Of course. May I ask who *does* know?'

'Megan and Tal Griffiths, naturally. Fortunately my condition wasn't discovered immediately, so the rescue team didn't find out. I was taken to a private hospital, where a consultant diagnosed the blindness as temporary.' Bran turned his face until he seemed to be staring straight into Naomi's eyes. 'As you can see I've been lucky—no lasting damage to my face, apart from the scar, which is the least of my worries. Vanity isn't one of my failings. The eye man assures me that gradually, bit by bit, I'll begin to see again. I bloody well hope he's right. In the meantime, to avoid going stark, staring mad, I agreed to do this autobiography.' He smiled sardonically. 'Not merely to alleviate boredom, of course. Only an idiot would have refused the advance Diadem offered.'

Naomi gazed numbly into his eyes, which were deep-set and ringed with lashes as thick as one of his sable brushes. The shock of his blindness was forgotten for the moment as she saw that instead of being dark as

26

she'd assumed, Bran Llewellyn's eyes were purest pale green, with a glitter which made the blindness hard to believe.

'You certainly don't talk much,' he said drily.

'I couldn't think of anything to say,' said Naomi, suppressing a shiver. Blindness in any form to anyone was terrible. But to an artist it was a disaster of cataclysmic proportions.

'You're honest, I'll say that for you!' His mouth twisted. 'Has my handicap lessened your enthusiasm for the job?'

Since she'd never had any enthusiasm for it in the first place Naomi felt it made very little difference, other than deepening her guilt about being in Bran Llewellyn's home under false pretences.

'Not at all. I shall be only too glad to help in any way,' she said neutrally. 'Perhaps you'd tell me where I'm to work——'

'You needn't get down to it right away—I'm not that much of a slavedriver!'

'As you wish. I just thought it would save time in the morning, when I do start.' Naomi got to her feet, wondering what she should do next, somewhat startled when Bran, sensing her indecision, told her to do what she liked before joining him for dinner.

'You've got until seven-thirty. Normally I eat later than that, but I thought we'd make it a rule to eat early, to allow for the reading session afterwards.'

'Thank you.' Inwardly Naomi was dismayed. She'd hoped for a tray in her room.

'Something's wrong again,' stated Bran. 'Odd, really. When I could see I rarely noticed people's reactions. Now they fairly vibrate in the air. Or maybe it's just your wavelength I'm tuned into, Naomi Barry. Are you pretty?' he added, startling her.

'No.'

'Modest! Describe yourself, then.' He turned his face in her direction, his mouth curved in a mocking smile.

She obeyed reluctantly. 'I'm smallish, hair and eyes brown; skin olive.'

'What are you wearing?'

'White shirt, yellow sweater, blue jeans.'

'How about your feet?'

Taken aback for a moment, Naomi reminded herself that he was an artist, that colour was his life. 'Yellow socks, navy deck-shoes, white laces and soles.'

'Good. You appreciate my need to see.' His nostrils twitched. 'You smell good, too.'

Colour flared, unseen, in Naomi's cheeks. 'I'm relieved.'

He shook his head impatiently. 'I meant your perfume. I detest heavy, musky scents. Yours is flowery, subtle.'

'Christmas present.'

'Do you always talk in shorthand?'

'I'm nervous.'

'What's making you nervous—apart from the obvious?' Bran paused, raising a sardonic eyebrow. 'Could it be you're worried about eating with me?'

'Not—not worried, exactly. I just assumed I'd have a tray in my room.'

This time the smile was bitter. 'Have no fear. Megan makes sure I get food I can cope with, so I don't slobber.'

Naomi could have kicked herself. 'That never occurred to me—honestly!'

'Then what the devil *is* bothering you?'

The fact that she was here at all was bothering her, she thought miserably. She'd hated the idea of infiltrating Bran Llewellyn's private retreat when she thought he was in full possession of his faculties. Now she felt like the lowest kind of criminal. But, knowing a confession would have him booting her out of Gwal-y-Ddraig a lot faster than she'd entered it, Naomi braced herself to give him some acceptable reason for her uneasiness.

'I just hope I'll be able to do the work efficiently enough to suit you, that's all,' she said lamely.

'Which is not the real reason, but obviously the only one I'm likely to get.' He shrugged. 'Perhaps you feel my manner's too personal on such short acquaintance. If so, don't blame the blindness, Naomi. I'm like that anyway. I've never believed in wasting time where women are concerned.'

'So I've heard,' said Naomi before she could stop herself.

'Ah, my reputation's gone before me, as usual. In which case I'm surprised you had the temerity to apply for the job.'

'So am I,' she blurted, then blushed fierily as his mouth curved again in a smile which raised the hairs on the back of her neck.

'Have no fear, Naomi. You'll be perfectly safe with me — if you want to be.' He turned his head as a clock outside in the hall chimed six. 'Saved by the bell. Go for a walk or have a bath, or take a nap, do whatever you like until dinnertime. I'll see you at seven-thirty.'

'May I make a request, please?' she asked stiffly.

'By all means.'

'Could I make two phone calls? My parents and my sister would like to know I've arrived safely.' She smiled wryly, forgetting he couldn't see. 'Their faith in my driving isn't very strong.'

'Ring anyone you like at any time, Naomi. Most rooms here have an extension.'

Naomi thanked him politely, then went off to make a short, reassuring phone call to her parents. After-

wards she rang Diana, left a brief message on her
sister's answering machine, then made a cup of tea
from the tray while she took stock of her meagre
wardrobe.

Diana, who'd suffered increasing pangs of conscience as the day for her sister's departure
approached, had begged to pay for some new clothes,
but Naomi wouldn't hear of it.

'I'm going to work, not socialise,' she'd said firmly.
'You can lend me one of your silk shirts, if you like,
and maybe a sweater, but that's it.'

Consequently it took very little time to choose
something suitable to wear down to dinner that first
evening. Not, she thought with a pang, that it mattered
how she looked. Bran could neither see her, nor had
any idea that he ever had. Once. Naomi smiled ruefully. If he wanted a description of her clothes all the
time he'd soon get bored. After the first few days
there'd be nothing new to report. She grinned at
herself in the mirror as she brushed her damp hair into
shape, realising she was taking unusual care with her
appearance just the same. Which only went to prove
how charismatic the man was, sighted or not. Her first
real look into those sea-green eyes had given her a jolt
like an electric shock. No wonder he mowed the ladies
down! Not, of course, that there was the slightest
possibility of joining the ranks of the mown where she
was concerned. If those green eyes were functioning
normally he'd know she wasn't his type at all. On the
other hand there was no one else for him to sharpen
his sexual claws on at this particular moment in time,
a fact which counselled caution. The man was everything she'd known he'd be, Naomi thought, depressed.
His powerful sexual appeal would have been danger-
ous enough normally, but in some strange way the

unexpected trauma of blindness, far from lessening it, only made it all the more lethal.

A knock on the door sent Naomi hurrying to find Megan outside on the landing.

'There's nice you look, Miss Barry,' said the house-keeper in admiration.

'Naomi, please!'

'Right you are.' Megan came into the room, looking apologetic. 'I hope you've made yourself some tea. I felt terrible not giving you some downstairs straight away, but Bran wanted to meet you as soon as possible, and wouldn't let me serve tea in the garden-room.' She sighed heavily. 'Didn't want you to watch him fumble with it, you see.'

'I quite understand,' Naomi assured her. 'I made myself tea up here, and couldn't resist those biscuits in the tin. You made them?'

'Yes indeed. Bran's favourites. Dinner in ten min-utes, then. Bran will be waiting in the dining-room— the door on the left across the hall.' Megan hesitated, eyeing Naomi anxiously. 'Think you'll get on with him all right?'

'Perhaps it's more a case of will he get on with me?' said Naomi ruefully, then smiled. 'I'll do my best, anyway.'

Megan looked at her thoughtfully, then nodded. 'Yes. I'm sure you will. I worry about him, you see. Terrible thing to happen.' She sighed deeply. 'Now I'd better get back to that dinner. I hope you enjoy it.'

'I will. I'm not much of a cook myself, but I appreciate good food.'

'Plenty of that here,' Megan assured her, and hur-ried off to see to it.

Naomi waited until the ten minutes were up, leaning at the window to gaze down the valley at the effect of sunset on the rounded, multi-tinted mountains. When she finally left the room to go downstairs, it was with an air of Daniel making a second visit to the lion's den.

Bran Llewellyn's garden-room had been furnished with a leaning to austerity only slightly relieved by the odd opulent touch. But his dining-room was the exact opposite. Naomi paused on the threshold, her eyes widening at the exuberance of carved mahogany furniture and heavy velvet curtains held back by great silk ropes thick enough to secure an ocean liner. An old, dim mirror in a heavily gilded frame hung over the fireplace, a pair of similarly framed oils hung on walls the tint of the terracotta pot which housed a flourishing palm. On the polished boards of the floor lay a rug in faded tints of coral and blue and sand, so exquisite that Naomi hardly liked to set foot on it.

Bran Llewellyn was already seated at the head of the table, his back to one of the pair of windows which overlooked the view Naomi could see from her bedroom. By his side stood a small, wiry man who said a quiet word to his employer as Naomi hesitated on the threshold.

'Come in,' ordered Bran. He raised an eyebrow as her heels clicked on the polished boards before sinking into the carpet. 'Not deck-shoes tonight, then?'

'No,' said Naomi. 'Though I think they'd be kinder to this carpet than heels. Good evening.' She held out her hand to the man beside Bran. 'How do you do? I'm Naomi Barry.'

'And this is Taliesin Griffiths,' said Bran as the quiet, smiling man shook Naomi's hand. 'For the time being he's working overtime, doubling as my eyes as well as driving me about and overseeing the garden.'

'Pleased to meet you, miss,' said Tal, and held out a chair for Naomi before going quietly from the room.

'I didn't get up when you came in,' said Bran

brusquely. 'I'm not very clever at all this yet. I knock things over.'

Naomi looked at the place settings, surprised that no allowances had been made for his blindness. The wine glasses were tall goblets, and the array of silverware was formidable.

'You're very quiet,' commented Bran.

'I was just wondering if it wouldn't be easier for you if there were less glass and cutlery and so on.'

'Of course it would,' he said impatiently. 'But I categorically refuse to make concessions. It's taken me most of my life to aspire to any luxury, and I intend to enjoy it, blind or not. Do you find that bloody-minded?'

'Not in the least. I admire you for it.'

'I'm not seeking admiration,' he said shortly. 'Tal says there's a minute or two to go before the meal arrives so tell me what you're wearing.'

'Are you going to ask that every time we meet?' she enquired. 'If so you'll soon get bored. My wardrobe's very limited.'

His mouth tightened. 'You think I'm rude. But I do the same with Megan and Tal, until Megan tells me off because she invariably wears a navy dress in the afternoons and gets tired of saying so. It's just that I'm cursed with this hunger to *see* everyone in my mind.'

Naomi felt a sharp pang of sympathy as she tried to view her clothes with an artist's eye. 'I'm wearing a saffron-yellow silk shirt and a narrow, shortish linen skirt—black, with a narrow suede belt through the waist loops. My shoes are suede too, with heels, and my earrings are silver filigree and fake topaz, sort of pear-shaped. My ears are pierced,' she added.

'Well done. Thank you.' Bran raised his head in the gesture she was coming to recognise. 'Dinner approaches.'

Tal served the first course. In the middle of each green plate lay a small crystal bowl containing mayonnaise redolent with garlic, and ringed round it were shelled Dublin Bay prawns, palely pink and succulent. Tal shook out a folded linen napkin and put it across Bran's knees, poured pale gold wine into the glasses then left them to their meal.

'Description isn't necessary at this point,' said Bran, and dipped the first prawn into the sauce with care. 'I know exactly how Megan serves these, so I can see the food quite clearly, which heightens the pleasure of eating to an amazing extent. Incidentally,' he added, popping the prawn into his mouth, 'Megan's mayonnaise is pretty lively, so if you're not a garlic-lover, beware.'

'I adore the stuff,' said Naomi indistinctly, her mouth full. 'Mmm, wonderful.' She watched, her heart in her throat, as Bran's long, sinewy hand reached out for a goblet and conveyed wine to his mouth without spilling a drop. He drank deeply, returned the glass to its exact location, then went on eating in silence for a moment.

'No applause?' he said at last.

Naomi choked on a mouthful of prawn. She drank some wine hastily, less deft by far than Bran as she replaced her glass. 'Applause?' she queried, playing for time.

'Don't pretend you weren't riveted by my performance with the wine glass, Naomi!'

'All right, then, I was *deeply* impressed! Will that do?' she said tartly, then bit her lip.

'Now what's the matter?' he asked impatiently.

'I'm sorry——'

'That I'm blind?'

'No. For the familiarity. Normally I'd be more polite. I apologise.'

'By normally, you mean if I could see.'

She thought it over. 'Well, yes — yes, I suppose I do mean that.'

'Don't sound so guilty.' Bran despatched the last prawn, then wiped his fingers on his napkin and turned his face in her direction. 'Let's get one thing clear, Naomi. I'm paying you to do a job for me, but I don't expect deference, or allowances for my handicap. We'll be thrown together far more than if we'd met in the usual way, but because our time together will be brief it seems only practical to take a few short-cuts. Here endeth the lesson.' He raised his head. 'Our next course is on its way. Not only do I hear the faint rattle of dishes, I can smell Megan's special beef casserole.'

'Is your sense of smell more acute now?' asked Naomi matter-of-factly.

'It seems to be. My hearing, too. It'll be interesting to see if they remain as sharp when I can see again. If I ever can.'

This time Megan accompanied Tal, in charge of a heated trolley as her huband removed the plates from the first course. She beamed as Naomi complimented her on the food.

'Thank you. I hope you feel the same after this lot, too.' Deftly she served Bran with tiny potatoes and small whole carrots, along with a creamy, fragrant helping of beef casserole, then put the dishes in front of Naomi for her to help herself. Tal refilled Bran's wine glass, gave Naomi the mineral water she requested instead, made sure everything was in its exact place in front of his employer, then went off with his wife to the kitchen.

Naomi gave herself a modest portion of everything and fell to with enthusiasm. 'Heavenly flavour,' she said rapturously.

Bran's mouth twitched at the corners. 'You like your food!'

'Too much, unfortunately. If I eat like this all the time I'm here I'll be dieting all summer afterwards.'

'So you're not the type who picks daintily at a lettuce leaf and dismisses puddings as the work of the devil?'

'Far from it. I share a flat with a really good cook, too,' said Naomi sighing.

'Male or female?'

Naomi stiffened. 'Female, as it happens.'

'Ah, I trespassed!'

She made no attempt to deny it as she watched his efficient way with his meal for a moment in silence.

'Lost in admiration again?' he enquired.

'Yes,' she said simply.

He aimed an unsettling smile in her direction. 'You know, Naomi, I'm beginning to think it was a lucky day for me when you applied for the job.'

She put down her fork, her appetite suddenly gone. 'You don't know that for certain.'

'Nothing's for certain,' he said with sudden bitterness. 'I can't even push my plate away in a temper, in case I knock something over, dammit.'

'Won't you have some more?'

He shook his head. 'Megan makes great puddings, I'll save myself for that, but you go ahead.'

'No, thanks. I'd like some pudding too.' Glad he couldn't see how much of her meal she'd left, Naomi rose to take their plates, careful not to disarrange anything in Bran's vicinity.

'Shall I ring that little bell?' she asked.

'No. Not yet. Let's just sit a little before Megan comes. You didn't eat much after all,' he added, startling her.

'I — I left some room for pudding. Clare and I make

do with a one-dish supper as a rule. We eat a lot of pasta. Which accounts for the unwanted bulges.'

'You don't sound like a girl who bulges.'

'So far I don't, too much. And I don't qualify for the term "girl" exactly, either. I'm twenty-seven.'

'I know. I learned that from your tape.'

'I thought you couldn't remember.'

'I lied. I wanted to hear you say it all again.' He shrugged. 'Twenty-seven sounds pretty young to someone of my advanced years.'

'Not all that advanced! It's common knowledge that you're a mere ten years older than me.'

His smile was bitter. 'Only in fact. In experience I'm probably twice your age.'

Naomi flashed a look at him, forgetting he couldn't see. 'My voice is obviously misleading. No one gets to my age completely unscathed!'

'I stand rebuked.' Bran's head went up. 'Our pudding's on the way.'

Megan came into the room with a tray, casting a disapproving look at the half-empty plates on the trolley. 'Wasn't it nice, then?'

'It was wonderful,' said Naomi hastily, 'but I was greedy with the first course, and I'm told you make irresistible puddings.'

Mollified, Megan set plates in front of them. 'Well, this coconut parfait's nice and light, and the passion-fruit sauce is good. Bran will vouch for that.'

'Very true,' he agreed, and reached unerringly for a dessertspoon. 'Normally, of course, I'd be posh and use a fork, but ——'

'But if you did you'd waste that sauce!' said Megan. 'I'll put coffee in the garden-room.'

'Thank you, Megan.' Bran blew a kiss in her general direction and the cheerful woman laughed as she trundled the trolley from the room. He went on talking easily as they finished the exquisite parfait, then at last he laid down the spoon and turned his head in Naomi's direction. 'Now for the awkward bit. Shall I call Tal, or are you up to navigating me back to the garden-room?'

'I'll do my best,' she assured him, her heart in her mouth as he pushed back the carver chair and stood upright, using the arms for guides. When Bran was erect he held out his hand and Naomi hurried to take it, the impact of his hard, warm fingers touching off an unwelcome chain reaction along her nerve-endings as she steered him round the table and across the carpet to the door.

'At this point,' he remarked, 'much as I like holding your hand, I can manage the rest of the journey alone. I don't deal in false pretences.'

Naomi's stomach muscles contracted as though he'd hit her. She swallowed hard, and excused herself on the pretext of needing something from her room. She left the tall, slow-moving man to find his own way, and escaped to her bedroom to stare in the mirror, breathing rapidly as she met her hunted eyes in despair. This was going to be so *hard*. It had been bad enough to learn Bran was blind, without discovering that one touch of his hand was enough to turn her to jelly. She waited until she'd pulled herself together, then smoothed her hair and went from the room to join her new employer.

Bran was sitting in his usual chair beside the fireplace in the garden-room. He turned his head as she knocked and went in.

'You were a long time.'

'I'm sorry. How do you like your coffee?'

'Black, strong and sweet.'

In silence Naomi half filled a large breakfast cup,

stirred in the sugar and handed cup and saucer to Bran, then poured coffee for herself and sat down.

'I know one should drink it from a *demi-tasse*,' he went on casually, 'but this size is easier for me. Thank you for not overfilling it.'

Naomi nodded, then bit her lip. 'I keep forgetting you can't see. I nodded.'

'You'll have to learn to say yes — when the question merits it, of course,' he added, smiling crookedly.

'I'll try to remember.'

'I sense a feeling of unease, Naomi. Is socialising with me a strain?'

'No! Not in the least.' Naomi cast about in her mind hurriedly for some way of convincing him she meant it. 'In fact I was just thinking I wouldn't be coping nearly as well if I were you.'

The lines on his face deepened abruptly. 'Ah, but I'm not always like this. Tonight I'm on my best behaviour, with a guest to show off for. But other times the darkness drives me mad. I get claustrophobic, desperate to see the light again —— ' He stopped abruptly, shrugging. 'A touch of Celtic melodrama to gain sympathy.'

'What do you miss most?' she asked, getting up to take his cup.

He laughed shortly. 'I'd probably shock you if I told you.'

'I doubt it.'

'I shan't try, then.' He relaxed a little, leaning his head back against the chair. 'Apart from the obvious lack of my work, I miss reading. If I was sure I'd never see again I suppose I'd start learning Braille, get a guide dog. But the way things are I can't settle to anything therapeutic. In any case all this is relatively recent. I've just about mastered crossing a room without blundering into the furniture.' He paused.

'That's a point. Don't move anything. I've got a rough plan of the downstairs rooms in my mind, and I can get up the stairs in the studio to my own bed, but my proficiency depends on everything remaining exactly as it is. So for the time being there are no vases of flowers about, and no small scatter rugs to trip me up.'

Naomi eyed the strong, brooding profile for a moment. 'Would it be any help,' she asked tentatively, 'if I read to you? Or wouldn't that be the same?'

Bran turned his face in her direction, frowning. 'Are you sure you want to do that?'

'Yes. I could make a start with the morning paper, read a headline or two, then you could choose which item you wanted read in detail. Unless you prefer the radio, of course.'

'Up to now I've had no choice,' he said thoughtfully. 'Maybe I'll take you up on your offer. We could give it a try in the morning and see how it goes. If it's too much for you I can always revert to Radio Four.'

Naomi put her cup back on the tray, wondering if this was the moment to withdraw discreetly and spend the rest of the evening in her room. Once again Bran read her mind.

'Now you don't know whether to stay, or to go to bed,' he observed.

'Yes.'

'Ah! You learn quickly.' He shrugged indifferently. 'If you're tired, by all means go to bed.'

'I'm not in the least tired.' She hesitated. 'What I'd really like is a look at where I'm going to work tomorrow and, if it's not asking too much, a visit to your studio.'

Bran rose with care. 'Come with me, then.' He led the way from the room slowly, but with a sureness which made it hard to believe he couldn't see his way. Naomi followed him across the hall, past the dining-room and through a doorway into a narrow corridor with a pair of double doors at the far end.

'This used to be a barn back in the past, when Gwal-y-Ddraig was a farm,' he said, when they reached the doors. He opened one, fumbled for light switches on the wall, and Naomi gasped as he revealed a room with a thirty-foot ceiling. The north wall and the portion of ceiling which sloped to meet it consisted entirely of windows, with a dais in front of them, and near by an easel with a half-finished portrait of a young woman. Canvases were everywhere, some piled on the floor, others hung, framed, on the stone walls, along with drawings and sketches Naomi itched to examine. At the back of the room a spiral stair led to a gallery furnished with a bed, and in the niche below it a Chinese screen painted with flying storks sheltered an old brocade sofa draped with a length of figured russet velvet. Several large, battered tables stood in the central portion of the room, littered with every item of paraphernalia an artist could possibly need.

'Well?' demanded Bran, moving closer to her. 'What's the verdict?'

'It's like the first act of *La Bohème*,' said Naomi without thinking. 'The only thing missing is a stove for Rudolfo to burn his play.'

'Clever girl. I based my designs for the recent Welsh National Opera production on it. You like opera?'

Naomi bit her lip, glad he couldn't see her scarlet cheeks. 'Some of them. The more tuneful ones.'

'You must listen to some of my recordings, then. Music, as you can imagine, is a godsend under my present circumstances.'

'Would you mind if I looked round?' she asked shyly. 'I've only seen reproductions of your work up to now.'

'Feel free.' Bran moved between the tables without

once touching anything, and sat down on the sofa while Naomi explored the spectacular room. She moved slowly between the four canvases hung on the walls. Two of them were landscapes, both of them menacing with approaching storm, in contrast to a seascape which conveyed warmth and high summer, with golden cliffs and a transparent aquamarine sea. But the fourth canvas brought Naomi to a standstill, her eyes wide as they met those in the self-portrait of the artist.

It was a head and shoulders study of a younger Bran Llewellyn, the bare torso depicted with a skill which paid full homage to every nerve, sinew and muscle beneath the skin. The eyes, green and watchful as a Welsh mountain cat, stared from beneath slightly frowning brows, the mouth set as though the artist's teeth were clenched tightly in concentration.

'You haven't moved for the last few minutes,' commented Bran. 'What are you looking at?'

'Your self-portrait,' she said quietly, turning in his direction. 'I've seen photographs of some of your other work, but not of that.'

'For the simple reason that no one in the art world knows it exists.' His mouth turned down at the corners. 'Rembrandt painted himself so often because it was cheaper than hiring models, but I feel no urge to reproduce my own face. I painted myself just once because my mother asked me to. When she died the portrait came back here. And here it stays. I prefer models with rather more interesting faces.'

Naomi, privately of the opinion that no face she'd seen in her entire life was more interesting than Bran Llewellyn's, said nothing as she moved towards the painting on the easel. Unlike his celebrated studies of gnarled and battered age, the woman in the portrait was young and flawlessly beautiful. Even in its half-finished state the work was magnificent. Pale gold hair and fair translucent skin were saved from insipidity by dark, slate-blue eyes which looked out on the world with supreme confidence. This girl, thought Naomi, never had a self-doubt in her life.

'I assume you're looking at Allegra,' said Bran. 'What do you think of her?'

'Very lovely.'

'Your tone suggests reservations.'

'Not about your skill. I just wish I had half her glittering self-confidence.'

'I was successful in capturing her, then. Allegra's nothing if not confident.'

'What woman wouldn't be with looks like hers?'

'Are yours so unsatisfactory to you?'

'My face wouldn't launch a thousand ships, certainly. Why is the portrait unfinished?' she added, changing the subject.

'I was about to complete it when the accident happened. My just desserts, I suppose. I took off on a climbing weekend instead of finishing the job.'

'She came here to sit for you?'

'No—to my studio in London. Daddy commissioned the painting. Daughter fell in love with the artist—and vice versa. Artist blinded, Allegra no longer interested. End of story.'

'But surely she knows it's only a temporary condition?'

'She's convinced it's permanent.' Bran's face set in bitter lines. 'I should be grateful. Allegra's shortcomings are much easier to see now I'm blind. Not that I blame her too much. I find it hard to believe in the temporary bit myself.'

'But you must believe in it,' said Naomi quickly.

'Then of course I will!' He rose to his feet. 'Let's move back to the study. Which is a rather grand name

for the cubbyhole which houses the word processor.'
He waited until Naomi joined him. 'I assume you can
use one?'

She laughed a little. 'I nodded again. I keep
forgetting.'

'Gratifying! Will you put the lights out?'

She complied, then stood still with her eyes closed
before opening the door.

'What are you doing?' he asked curiously.

'Standing with my eyes shut, trying to imagine what
it's like for you.'

There was silence for a moment. 'You're a strange
girl, Naomi Barry,' he said slowly, the lilt in his voice
very much in evidence.

'Not really.' She opened the doors into the dimly lit
corridor. 'In normal circumstances I wouldn't be so —
so informal.'

'But because I'm blind and you're temporary we've
bypassed several of the preliminaries which inhibit
newly acquainted people.'

'Exactly.'

He sent a wry, sardonic smile her way, then pre-
ceded her along the corridor towards a door Naomi
hadn't noticed earlier. Bran reached a hand inside and
fumbled slightly for the light, revealing a small, very
functional room.

'Until last week this was a sort of store cupboard.
Now it's your new domain.'

Naomi sniffed at the smell of fresh paint as she
inspected the word processor enthroned on a plain
pine desk. Otherwise the room held only a couple of
office chairs, a small side-table, and shelves containing
typing paper, a thesaurus, a dictionary, and a cassette
player. Bran informed her that the window looked out
over the back garden and the small wing where the
Griffithses lived in rooms above the kitchen.

'No one's likely to disturb you here,' he added. 'Will it do?'

'Admirably.'

'Good. Have a nightcap before you go to bed.'

'If you don't mind I'll just go straight up.' Naomi gave a rueful little chuckle. 'For the record, I'm giving you an apologetic smile.'

Bran stopped so suddenly that Naomi bumped into him. His hands shot out to steady her, but dropped the moment she regained her balance. 'Sorry. I didn't realise you were so close. I just wanted to say how much I appreciate your attitude. People tend to treat me like part of my porcelain collection.'

'Anything less like a piece of china would be hard to imagine,' she assured him.

Bran leaned in the doorway, blocking her way. 'Naomi, would you do something for me?'

She eyed him warily. 'If I can.'

'Just this once, would you let me touch your face? Your bone-structure will give me some idea of the way you look.'

'If you wish,' she said reluctantly.

Naomi did her best to stand still as Bran reached out to touch her. His long, spatulate artist's fingers moved with delicacy over her brow and nose and along her cheekbones, exploring the lines of her jaw and the length of her nose, light and fleeting on the curve of her mouth, but trailing a line of fire along her nerves in their wake. Her relief was intense when he moved his hand to her hair, running a tress of it through his fingers before he stood back.

'Thank you. I'd pictured you with shorter, straighter hair.'

'It just waves a bit at the ends.' Naomi stayed where she was, hoping he couldn't tell how much his exploration had disturbed her.

'You're embarrassed,' he said, standing aside for her to pass. 'Don't worry, Naomi, I won't repeat the exercise. But I can't believe you're not pretty. Your bones are beautiful.'

She eyed him uncertainly as they arrived in the hall. 'That's an odd sort of compliment.'

'From me it's the highest possible praise!' He held out his hand, and with some misgiving she grasped it with her own. 'So, Naomi.' He smiled enigmatically. 'You've come safely to the end of your first day at Gwal-y-Ddraig. Do you think you'll survive "amid the alien corn"?'

CHAPTER THREE

Despite the rigours of the drive from London and the testing evening in the company of Bran Llewellyn, Naomi found it hard to sleep that first night at Gwal-y-Ddraig. Guilt at the deception she was practising, worse than ever now she'd met Bran, battled with another emotion as disturbing as it was unexpected. Aghast at her own response to Bran Llewellyn's famous attraction, she lay awake for hours, knowing that she should make some excuse to leave this beautiful place right away. She tried to soothe her conscience by assuring it she was obliged to stay to help Diana, that she was committed now to helping Bran, too. But the truth was more basic. Now she'd met Bran she had no wish to leave a moment before she had to, a fact which kept sleep at bay almost until dawn. When Naomi woke again, only an hour or two later, she found rain sheeting down outside and the Black Mountains of Gwent living up to their description.

Afraid that seven in the morning was on the early side to go in search of breakfast, she had a leisurely bath, dressed in the same jeans and sweater as the day before, and took time in choosing socks to match her blue chambray shirt. She smiled crookedly. Bran's thirst for pictorial detail was affecting her already. She made her bed, tidied the room, then went downstairs, drawn by the scent of bacon towards a door in the alcove under the staircase. She knocked and entered the kitchen, smiling apologetically when she found Tal

47

and Megan seated at one end of a large scrubbed table, finishing what looked like a very substantial breakfast.

They both sprang up, but Naomi waved them back to their seats, embarrassed.

'Good morning—please don't let me interrupt. I wasn't sure what I was supposed to do.'

'Come in, come in,' said Megan, smiling, her husband quieter but no less welcoming as he returned Naomi's greeting and began to clear away. 'There's early you are. I was just going to bring you a tray.'

Naomi shook her head vigorously. 'No, indeed! Couldn't I just eat in here?'

The other two exchanged looks doubtfully. 'Bran said you were to have a tray in your room,' said Tal. 'That's what he does, you see, miss. He's not at his best in the mornings.'

'I'd much rather come down,' said Naomi firmly.

Megan jumped up and began clearing dishes. 'If you're sure, then. I'll just put some bacon on for you.'

'I never eat a cooked breakfast——' began Naomi, then stopped. 'On the other hand it does smell wonderful. Could I just have some in a sandwich?'

The kitchen was big, and even on a dull, rainy morning it was welcoming and warm, with plants on the windowsills, and herbs hanging from hooks ranged along the central beam of the ceiling. Naomi was soon provided with a sandwich made from wholemeal bread and crisp, flavoursome bacon, and ate with appreciation, as Tal laid a tray and made toast to accompany the scrambled eggs Megan crowned with a silver cover.

'You've forgotten the paper——' Megan stopped, biting her lip, and Tal patted her shoulder.

'There, there, love. None of us is used to it yet, Bran most of all. I'll go up and see to him.'

Megan brought over the pot of tea Naomi had asked for, and sat down at the table to share it with her. 'It's terrible, terrible,' she said tearfully, and swiped at her eyes with a corner of her apron. 'Thank the lord his poor mother's not alive to see him like this.'

Naomi leaned over and touched her hand sympathetically. 'But the blindness is only temporary, Megan. Mr Llewellyn said so.'

Megan nodded, sniffing. 'Yes, I know. And if praying will make his sight come back he'll soon be all right, believe me. Not *his* prayers, of course. Mine.' She shot a searching look at Naomi. 'Are you wondering why Tal and I are on such familiar terms with him?'

Naomi smiled. 'I imagine you've known him a long time.'

'All his life! We knew his family well, you see, came from the same village in the Rhondda. His dad was a collier, like Tal, but had to come up the pit with dust.'

'Dust?' queried Naomi, frowning.

'Pneumoconiosis — coaldust in the lungs,' explained Megan. 'Mrs Llewellyn taught in the infants' school. Lovely woman she was. But they weren't young when Bran was born. Brangwyn he was christened, after Sir Frank, the man who painted the panels in the Brangwyn Hall in Swansea. But the boy had such a shock of dark hair when he was born his Dad said he looked like a little black crow — *bran* in Welsh — and that's what he's been ever since.'

Naomi listened, rapt, making a mental note of it for Diana. 'Was he the only child?'

'Yes, indeed. His mother was forty when Bran was born, caused quite a stir in the village!' Megan's face shadowed. 'But Huw Llewellyn died when Bran was a teenager and Olwen about ten years later. They didn't live to see their son's success. I think his dad was disappointed that Bran had no interest in teaching, or engineering. But all the boy ever wanted was to draw and paint, and in the end he showed everybody he was right, didn't he?'

'Has he lived in this house long?'

'No. Only a few years.' Megan smiled fondly. 'About the time he bought Gwal-y-Ddaig the colliery where Tal worked closed down, so Bran asked us if we'd like to come here and keep house for him.' She looked fierce suddenly. 'You don't want to believe all this rubbish they write about Bran in the papers — women and stuff, I mean. They throw themselves at him, that's the trouble. Bran can't help the looks God gave him.'

'For pity's sake, Megan,' said Tal, coming back into the room. 'Give it a rest.' He smiled apologetically at Naomi. 'She thinks the world of him.'

'And you don't!' scoffed Megan, unoffended, then eyed the tray with disapproval. 'He didn't eat much this morning.'

'Not one of his good days, love.' He turned to Naomi. 'He says he'll leave you in peace this morning, miss, so you can get used to the machine on your own. He gave me a tape for you. I've left it on your desk.'

Deeply grateful to Bran Llewellyn for leaving her alone for her first morning, Naomi quickly familiarised herself with the equipment, but found it difficult at first to coordinate her typing to the deep, musical voice on the tape. In time she managed to adjust the tape to a speed slow enough for her to work at a comfortable rate, and settled to the task. Naomi smiled when she heard that the title was to be *The Flight of the Crow*, wondering if she should tell him she knew the reason for his choice. Not that Bran Llewellyn could object to Megan's confidences, which were only a rather more colourful version of the facts Bran was telling her on the tape. For a time Naomi concentrated on just transposing the spoken word to the screen, but after a while her absorption in Bran's story was so intense that her fingers were soon flying over the keys of their own volition.

Naomi was so lost to the world that she jumped yards when a hard, warm hand descended on her shoulder, sending a shiver down her spine. She spun round to see Bran Llewellyn shaking his head at her.

'I know you're in a hurry to get the job done, Naomi Barry, but Megan tells me you've been at it for hours. It's time you knocked off for a bit.'

Naomi blinked owlishly, swallowing a yawn as she wished him good morning. 'I didn't realise it was so late.'

'Nice to have something to pass the time so quickly,' he said dourly. 'Come on. Megan's taken a tray of coffee to the studio.'

'But couldn't I just have it here?' she asked, looking longingly at the screen.

'*No*. Take a break.' Bran felt for the door and left, taking it for granted she was following behind, but Naomi paused to write the last page to disk, then made a hurried visit to the cloakroom in the hall.

'Right,' she said brightly, when she reached the studio. 'Coffee?'

'I can't pour it myself,' he said irritably.

Naomi's lips tightened as she handed him a cup of sweetened, strong black coffee. 'Biscuit?'

'No. Sit down. Relax. Your obvious yen to escape is bloody insulting!'

'You should be flattered,' said Naomi tartly.

'Why?'

'Because your story's so engrossing I can't wait to get back to it.'

Bran was silent for a moment, his head bowed over his cup as though it comforted him to feel the heat of the liquid on his face. He was dressed for the weather in moleskin trousers and a heavy fisherman's jersey, his feet in battered suede boots. 'How does it sound?' he asked morosely. 'Grammatically, and so on?'

'Good. Very good. But so far I've been too lost in what you're saying to worry about the way you're saying it. In any case I'll sort that out later before I print the first tape.'

'So you go for the rags-to-riches theme?' he asked sardonically, raising his head.

'Hardly that,' retorted Naomi, determined not to pander to his mood. 'You come from a highly respectable working-class background.'

'I was speaking metaphorically.'

'There's always appeal in the man of talent who works his way from obscurity to limelight, whatever field he specialises in.'

'Do you think the book will sell?'

'I've no idea. But your publisher must think so, otherwise you wouldn't have been offered a big advance,' she added bluntly.

Bran shrugged. 'I suppose you're right. But if they're expecting a kiss-and-tell epic, with lots of celebrity names peppered over the pages, they'll be disappointed. Besides, if I'd been to bed with half the women I've been accredited with I'd never have had the energy to lift a brush and there wouldn't be any story.'

Naomi's cheeks warmed. 'Perhaps you could limit yourself to those women who've provided inspiration — motivation, and so on.'

'Lately I've painted very few women at all — and then only when commissioned. I prefer to paint age, character, even suffering, morbid Celt that I am.'

Naomi turned swiftly to the painting on the easel.

'You're looking at Allegra,' he said at once.

'Yes. No age or suffering there.'

'I was — infatuated with Allegra.'

'It shows.'

'Nevertheless, go and look at that face more carefully, now you can see it in daylight.'

The weather had cleared by this time. A watery sun was breaking through the clouds, illuminating the portrait far more revealingly than the artificial light of the night before. The beautiful, assured face looked different. Naomi stood in front of the painting, hands behind her back, her eyes narrowed assessingly.

'Tell me what you see,' commanded Bran.

'The light makes a difference,' admitted Naomi. 'I took her to be younger than me. Now I'm not so sure.'

'Well done. Anything else?'

'Are you sure you want me to say more?'

'Yes. Be honest. Speak your mind.'

Naomi scrutinised the portrait closely. 'She looks — not spoilt exactly, but wilful, used to having her own way.'

'Go on.'

'I get the impression she's demanding, expects a lot.'

'Right on the button.' His mouth twisted bitterly. 'One of her demands being a lover with twenty-twenty vision.'

'Is it any good saying you're better off without someone like that?' said Naomi quietly.

'None whatsoever.'

She scowled, unseen. 'Time I got back to my desk.'

Bran waved a newspaper at her. 'First I thought I'd take you up on your offer to read. I heard an item in brief on the radio, and I'm curious.'

Naomi took hold of the paper as if it were red-hot, then sagged with relief as she found his taste ran to a more sober publication than the *Chronicle*. 'What do you want to know?'

'A Canaletto sold yesterday in London for a preposterously large sum. I'd like to hear the details.'

Naomi found the article and began to read, as interested as Bran Llewellyn in the sale. Afterwards they discussed it for a moment then Bran waved her off.

'All right, Naomi. I'll let you off any more until after dinner.'

'I'll have a chapter ready by then, maybe even two,' she promised as she made for the door.

'Just a minute,' said Bran peremptorily. 'What are you wearing today?'

'Nothing very different. Jeans, same yellow sweater, new blue shirt and socks.'

His mouth twisted. 'You must be cursing the day you answered my advertisement, Naomi.'

More than he knew, she thought, suppressing a shiver, glad he couldn't see her face. 'Whenever I flag I'll think of the money you're paying me,' she assured him, keeping her tone light.

'Is money important to you, then?'

'Only when I don't have any, which happens with monotonous regularity just before pay day.'

He frowned. 'Can't you find something more remunerative to do, for heaven's sake?'

'I like my job,' she said very precisely.

'And I should mind my own business!'

Naomi went back to her labours feeling that life at Gwal-y-Ddraig would prove even more wearing than anticipated if Bran Llewellyn was so quick to pick every nuance of her mood. It was something never encountered in a man before. Certainly not with Greg. She sat staring into space, praying that Bran's antennae weren't strong enough to detect this new, unwanted vulnerability on her part.

Lunch was served on a tray at her desk at her own

request. Bran, it seemed, would not be in evidence until dinnertime. Tal had taken him for a drive, as Megan said he did most days since the accident.

Naomi ate quickly, eager to edit and print the first chapter. It was well after five by the time she'd finished, after a reminder of the time from Megan. Bran, it seemed, had left instructions that Miss Barry wasn't to be allowed to work late.

'He said you're to go for a walk in the fresh air,' warned Megan. 'Oh, and by the way, your sister rang this afternoon, asking if you could call her back this evening. She wouldn't let me fetch you to the phone.'

Naomi was relieved Diana'd had the sense to wait until their talk was relatively private. Not that it would do to be careless, even so. The slightest suspicion of what she was up to, she knew, would have Bran packing her back where she came from at the speed of light.

In contrast to the morning the spring evening was so warm and sunny that Naomi enjoyed her stroll through the rambling gardens, which were on several levels, with retaining walls in the few places where the lawns were flat. Long ago in the past the owner who had first converted the farm to a private house had planted trees and laurel hedges to maximum effect. Now, in full maturity, they formed windbreaks and separate areas bounded by beech and conifer and horse-chest-nuts, with the bright peachy pink of Japanese maple in accent here and there. The bare branches of a liriod-endron, the tulip tree, towered above the shrubbery, marking the boundary of the largest lawn, which had stone seats either end for watching whatever game had once been played there. To her delight, beyond it Naomi discovered a wild, woodland portion dense with trees flourishing as nature intended among drifts of daffodils piercing a carpet of last year's leaves. Tal must have his work cut out, she thought in awe, as she took in the extent of the grounds in his care. Megan might well extol Bran Llewellyn's kindness, but the roles the Griffiths couple filled at Gwal-y-Ddraig were anything but sinecures.

Naomi had a bath and got ready for dinner before making the call to Diana.

'I got your message. I've been on pins waiting for you to call,' said her sister at once. 'Look, Naomi, I've changed my mind. I was a selfish pig to make you do this. I'm getting bad vibes about the whole thing, so make some excuse and come back right away.'

Naomi almost dropped the telephone. 'Now you tell me! Anyway, it's too late. I—I'm committed. Everyone here's very kind. I even have a telephone in my room like everyone else here,' she added significantly.

There was silence on the line for a moment. 'I see,' said Diana unhappily. 'Well, if you must stay, please take care.'

'You still have the same aim, I suppose?' asked Naomi guardedly.

'Well, yes. But only if it's feasible.'

'I'll do my best. See you when I get back to London.'

'Right. But, Naomi—please be careful.'

'Don't worry. I will.'

Naomi sat at the dressing-table when she'd put down the phone, jotting a few brief sentences in the note-book Diana had provided. Afterwards she locked it away in her suitcase, feeling like a criminal as she stowed the suitcase at the back of the wardrobe. She hadn't dared ask Diana exactly what was needed in case they were overheard, but one thing was certain. As no journalist had ever penetrated the environs of Gwal-y-Ddraig before, Diana could at least describe the house. But Bran Llewellyn's blindness was a secret Naomi had no intention of telling anyone.

When she went downstairs to join Bran in the dining-room he was slumped in his chair, a glass of whisky in front of him. His head rose as he heard her come in, his face morose as she seated herself at his right.

'Good evening,' said Naomi, eyeing him, aware at once that unlike his choice of clothes his mood was funereal.

Bran sat with long legs outstretched under the table, his fingers encircling the glass. He wore a corduroy jacket the colour of expensive claret, with a Prussian blue bandana knotted at the open collar of his cream linen shirt.

'Portrait of an artist,' he said with bitterness, sensing her scrutiny. 'One is expected to be colourful.'

Naomi leaned back in her seat. 'Are you in the habit of doing what's expected, then?'

His face relaxed slightly. 'No. Far from it. To be honest——'

'People usually follow that with a whopping big lie,' she said, hoping he could tell she was smiling.

'How right you are! Anyway, what I was about to say sounds like a plea for sympathy, so I won't say it.'

'Now I'm curious!'

He shrugged. 'It's just that I choose my clothes these days by the feel of them. Texture has suddenly assumed enormous proportions. I've had the clothes a long time, so I can picture the colours, but the real comfort comes from the smoothness of the silk scarf and the soft old corduroy. Can you understand that?'

'Very easily. I like the feel of good material against my skin myself.'

'I remember. You were wearing a silk shirt last night.'

'My sister lent it to me. And before you ask I'm

wearing it again tonight. The only variation is my earrings, which are ordinary pearl drops tonight.'

Bran's mood lightened visibly. He took a pull on his whisky, then turned to her. 'What would you like to drink?'

'There's some nice Welsh mineral water on the table. I'll help myself to that,' she said quickly. 'I don't drink much.'

'Because you can't afford it?'

'There is that, of course. But the main reason is a tendency to headaches if I drink more than one glass of wine.'

'Very inhibiting,' he said, amused, then raised his head. 'Dinner approaches. Good evening, Megan,' he called, 'what are you delighting us with tonight?'

Megan came into the room with a tray, chuckling. 'You love doing that, Bran Llewellyn. I was trying to be so quiet, too.'

'I'd know your fairy footsteps anywhere!' He sniffed as she put a dish down in front of him. 'What's this?'

'Melon in port wine. Nice little cubes — use your spoon.'

'Not too much port, I hope. Naomi has a low alcohol threshold.'

Naomi laughed. 'Not too low to manage this; it looks wonderful. Megan's very artistic with food,' she added once they were alone, then hesitated.

'What is it?' he asked instantly.

She must learn to be stricter with herself, she thought in dismay. 'Perhaps you should know that Megan told me one or two things about you this morning. She felt a stranger might wonder about her informality with you, so she told me how they came to work here.'

'It's not quite as philanthropic as it sounds. I could hardly manage here on my own.' His mouth twisted.

'I'd be lost without them at this particular juncture in my life, lord knows.'

For the rest of the meal he kept, very deliberately, to lighter, more impersonal topics of conversation, asking questions about Naomi's job, with particular interest in her knowledge of ceramics.

'You can bid for me at the next sale, Naomi. I always feel I'm getting fleeced over the phone.'

She assured him she'd be happy to bid for him, confident in the knowledge that when the next sale came up she'd be far away from Gwal-y-Ddraig, back where she belonged.

Later, in the garden-room, Naomi drank her coffee quickly so that she could begin reading the first chapter of *The Flight of the Crow*.

'I didn't finish two, after all,' she told Bran. 'I decided to go over this one thoroughly, then work on the next chapter tomorrow. With only forty thousand or so words of text it shouldn't take me long to finish anyway.'

'You're very eager to be up, up and away,' said Bran moodily. 'Is my company so wearing?'

'Not in the least,' said Naomi, not entirely truthfully. 'I'd merely like to spend a couple of days with my parents if I can before I get back to work in London.'

His face relaxed. 'Ah, I see. Right, then, Scheherazade. Read.'

Naomi took her time over the introduction to Bran Llewellyn's life-story, a red ballpoint at the ready for any alterations he might want. With a Welsh love of words as potent as his gift with the brush, Bran Llewellyn painted a very vivid picture of the small village where he was born, where the dominant factor was the colliery which had provided most of the inhabitants with their livelihood.

From its beginning in a slate-roofed, terraced household, Bran's childhood came through as one influenced by a respect for learning, with love and discipline in abundant supply. He received his first taste of education at the infants' school where his mother had taught for years before her late, unexpected marriage, though Olwen Llewellyn had made very sure her son could read and write long before his first lesson at a schooldesk. She also taught him to play the piano in the hope that music, in some form, would eventually be his career. 'Mam,' said Bran in his text, 'had high hopes of one day seeing me graduate as a doctor of music from Oxford.'

Not for Bran Llewellyn the artistic launchpad of grinding poverty and aggro from unsympathetic parents. Harmony in the Llewellyn household had been the stuff of everyday life, until the death of his father when Bran was in his teens. Abruptly the carefree, sunlit prologue to his life was over as the descent of his father's coffin into the grave had changed Bran Llewellyn from boy to adult in the space of one sombre, hymn-resonant afternoon.

'Well, what do you think?' asked Bran.

'I think it's excellent,' said Naomi. 'But is that how you want it to sound? I edited it a bit, but only to tighten it up in places. If you want to change anything, please say so.'

'I'm impressed. Whether it's my own literary style or your expertise I'm not quite sure, but it sounds pretty good so far.'

'*I* think it's very good. So is the next bit.' Naomi chuckled. 'Now you can see why I was so anxious to get back to it. I couldn't wait to see what happened next.' She glanced over at the grand piano in the corner of the room. 'Do you still play?'

Bran shrugged. 'Occasionally. I'm no virtuoso, but I play well enough to amuse. I was in great demand in college. My crowd hung out in a local with a piano, and the others used to stand me drinks as long as I made the night hideous with whatever was in the top ten. If they grew maudlin some of them would even settle for a bit of Debussy sometimes, but not often.'

'I'd settle for some Debussy, if you'd play for me,' said Naomi impulsively, then held her breath, expecting a snub.

To her surprise Bran got up. 'You're a glutton for punishment, Miss Scribe.'

He threaded his way expertly through the furniture to the open piano and sat down. He ran his fingers experimentally over the keys for a moment or two, then began to play.

Naomi sat still, hardly daring to breathe as the strains of 'Clair de Lune' crept softly through the room, then merged into 'The Girl with the Flaxen Hair', and on to Ravel and 'Pavane for a Dead Infanta'. Suddenly, with a great rippling *arpeggio* up and down the keys, Bran launched into a medley of Beatles songs, choosing the earlier, raucous tunes at first, then changing to the plaintive strains of 'She's Leaving Home'. The sad, subtle interpretation moved Naomi so deeply that she remained silent long after the last plangent note had died away.

'Still no applause, Naomi?' He returned to the sofa and leaned back, stretching his long legs out across the carpet. 'What a deflating creature you are, to be sure.'

'I didn't want to break the spell,' she said, clearing her throat. 'You play very well.'

'No. I play *quite* well. And that's as highbrow as I get. If you want Chopin and Liszt you'll have to resort to my record collection.'

'Was your mother very disappointed when you turned down music as a career option?'

'My mother was a very practical woman. When Dad

died it was obvious that I'd need a scholarship of some kind to get to college.' Bran shrugged his shoulders. 'When I got one to the Slade there were no more arguments. She couldn't see how I was going to make a living out of painting, but consoled herself with the fact that if necessary I could always teach, like her.' He turned in her direction, eyebrow raised. 'Naomi, pour me a whisky—please. Half and half with a lot of soda.'

She poured a generous measure of spirit into a tumbler, topped it up with soda, then took it back and put it in Bran's hand.

'Thank you. What *shall* I do without you when you leave?' he asked mockingly. 'You've only been here five minutes and already you're indispensable.'

'No one's indispensable.'

'Some more than others, Naomi.'

'By the time I leave you'll be able to see,' she said briskly. 'Now if you don't mind I'll say goodnight. I'm a little tired.'

'Not surprising. Working for me is no soft option, is it?'

'It makes a change from washing-up,' she said wryly.

Bran frowned blankly. 'Washing-up?'

'When my employer brings back a carload of china from a sale, who do you think washes the stuff?'

'Give me your hand.'

Bran's fingers moved over her palm, smoothing the skin.

'They don't feel like dishpan hands.'

'Rupert supplies us with handcream,' she said with difficulty, her entire body alight in response to his touch.

'Us?'

'His wife helps in the shop, with two part-timers at

weekends. The others do more washing than me, actually.'

'Why?'

'I keep the firm's books.'

'Capable creature! What else do you do with your life?'

'Not much. My life isn't really all that interesting,' she said, and pulled her hand away before his fingers could reach her racing pulse.

Bran gave a short, mirthless laugh. 'In my present state, Naomi, anything that breaks the monotony for me is interesting, even the brand of detergent you use to wash all this antique china!'

CHAPTER FOUR

NAOMI went up to her room that night a prey to several warring emotions. The sensible thing, she knew perfectly well, was to go back to London right away. The fact that she had no intention of doing so was nothing to do with helping Diana, either. She simply wanted to stay in Bran Llewellyn's vicinity for as long as it took to complete the book. It was useless to pretend she wasn't attracted to his abrasive, powerful personality, and had been from the moment she'd bumped into him at the opera. Even the shock of discovering he was blind had only added to the attraction, making him more accessible, somehow, more human. Naomi stood in the middle of her room and closed her eyes, trying hard to visualise what it was like to be condemned to darkness, when the very essence of life to Bran was colour and light and the gift to transfer what he saw to canvas.

She opened her eyes and came back to earth with a bump as she took the notebook from its hiding place. Dreams of Bran Llewellyn as anything but a temporary employer were pipedreams, whereas Diana was part of the fabric of her life, a loving supportive sister who for once needed help which Naomi could provide. If an inside story on the artist was what it took to get Diana her heart's desire, Naomi felt she owed it to her sister to help even if it risked bringing the wrath of Bran Llewellyn down on her own head in the process. Not that he need find out. He probably never read the *Chronicle*. Even if Diana did get the article printed he wouldn't see it. Nor would there be anything in it the least bit objectionable, Naomi consoled herself. She had no intention of passing on anything personal, other than a description of his house. The rest of it would soon be common knowledge in the autobiography, anyway, except for the blindness — and Allegra. And she had no intention of saying a word on either subject, to Diana or anyone else.

The next few days were very similar in routine; breakfast with Megan and Tal and an early start at the word processor, with a visit from Bran at coffee time, then no further meeting until their evening together.

Naomi's guilt diminished with surprising rapidity as she succumbed to the allure of life at Gwal-y-Ddraig, where the loudest noises came from the occasional swooping jet. Now lambing time was over even the sheep were less vocal. London receded into the background. Reality was life here with Bran Llewellyn in his remote, beautiful home in the Welsh Marches.

'Tomorrow is Saturday,' said Bran over dinner the following week. 'I vote we go out. You've been working without a break since you arrived and you need a day off. I'll get Tal to take us on a trip round the area. You can't go back to the city without a guided tour of the land of my fathers, Naomi Barry. We'll visit my favourite haunts and you shall describe them for me, let me see them through your eyes.'

'Oh, but — '

'But nothing. You can't do any more until I give you another tape, anyway, and I refuse to do that until Monday morning,' he said flatly, then his face darkened. 'You'll have Monday to yourself to work in peace. I'm off to the eye man for a check-up.'

Naomi's knife and fork clattered to her plate. 'Something wrong?'

'No. Just routine. Do I detect a note of sympathy?'

'Of course you do.'

His mouth twisted bitterly. 'Just make sure it's not pity, Naomi. That I object to—violently.'

'I'll try to remember,' she said tartly.

'Ah. Now I've annoyed you.'

'Yes, you have.'

'Which means you won't come tomorrow, I suppose.'

'Certainly not. I'd be silly to turn down an outing.'

'Such practicality!'

'A quality you admired in your mother.'

He snorted. 'True. You remind me of her. Often.'

'I'll take that as a compliment,' said Naomi, amused. 'Why do I remind you of your mother?'

'Like you, she had a tendency to cut me down to size.'

'I wouldn't dream of attempting any such thing!' Naomi folded her napkin. 'Now, if you've finished, I suggest we get on. I did more than usual today, so I'd like to make an early start on the reading.'

'Not before I finish my wine, woman!'

Naomi subsided. 'Oh, sorry. Shall I ask Megan to take the coffee to the garden-room?'

'No. I've a fancy to listen to you in the studio tonight.'

This prospect made Naomi uneasy. In the rest of the house she could forget what Bran's blindness meant to him. In the studio she was deeply conscious of his deprivation. Among the trappings of his craft the tragedy of his blindness was inescapable, honing her own conscience to the point where it cut deep with sudden, unwelcome reminders that however she felt about Bran she was, in essence, using him for her own ends. The fact that she was doing it to help Diana made it no better. In the end, thought Naomi cynically, as she went with Bran to the studio, what could one solitary article possibly do for her sister, anyway, other than boost her career a little? If Diana really believed it would make Craig Anthony fall in love with her she was deluding herself. Love just happened. Suddenly, sometimes. As she knew herself only too well. And just as suddenly it stopped and left you flat. Which brought her back full circle to Diana. Without her sister's love and support, thought Naomi bleakly, she'd have been in a sorry state after Greg walked out of her life.

'You seem distracted tonight,' remarked Bran, when they were sitting on the sofa together in the studio.

'I'm a bit tired, that's all. I worked a few minutes longer to finish a chapter.' Naomi leaned forward to pour coffee, careful, as always, as she handed a cup to Bran.

'I'll make sure Megan blows a whistle promptly at five if you persist in working overtime.' His mouth tightened. 'Your tearing hurry to escape is very bad for my ego, Naomi—what lure lies in London to make you so keen to get back there?'

'The lure of a steady job.'

'No possessive lover, lusting for your return?'

'My private life, Mr Llewellyn, is entirely my own business,' said Naomi quietly. 'Now can we get on, please?'

He replaced his cup on the coffee-tray with unerring accuracy, then sat back. 'In a minute. Tell me about this lover.'

Naomi got up. 'Since you're obviously in no mood for work——'

'Sit down!' He pointed an imperious finger in her direction. 'I decide when I'm not in the mood to listen, Naomi Barry, not you.'

She subsided, offended, and rustled the manuscript ostentatiously.

'All right, all right,' he said irritably. 'Stop bristling

and get on with the great work. If you must know, I'll
be as glad to finish the blasted thing as you are.'

Naomi began to read, her delivery stilted at first
because she was annoyed. But after a while she forgot
to be offended, seduced, as always, by the fascination
of Bran Llewellyn's struggle for fame. The autobiography had reached the stage where Bran was leading a
hand-to-mouth existence in Camberwell, reluctantly
dependent on subsidies from his mother to pay the
rent for his draughty attic studio. From the text it was
obvious that Bran Llewellyn had good reason to be
thankful in those early, striving days for the charisma
which persuaded more than one girl to model for him
for love.

'I can tell by your tone you're looking down your
nose,' he said challengingly.

'I'm not. You've already told me you never had to
pay for a model — not in money, anyway.'

'If you mean I conferred sexual favours in return for
a sitting, you're right.' He laughed. 'Though to be
honest, Naomi, I never saw it like that at the time. All
those romps with willing, generous young things were
just part and parcel of life and the urge to transfer my
inner vision to canvas, paper, anything I could lay my
hands on.'

Fortunately for Bran Llewellyn, his work had
excited interest even before he left college. His teach-
ers were unanimous in pronouncing him an accomplished, even brilliant draughtsman, and an early series
of pencil drawings of his mother and various inhabitants of the Welsh village of his birth had been sold
before he left the Slade. Then a famous actor,
impressed by the young Welshman's work, had asked
Bran to try his hand at a portrait. This had proved so
successful that it had brought in a flood of similar
commissions, but Bran Llewellyn had refused to suc-

cumb entirely to what Gainsborough described as 'This curs'd Face Business'. Landscapes were his true metier, and while sensual drawings of youthful models earned his bread and butter in his Camberwell days their main function for Bran had been to allow him to get on with an exhibition of oil-paintings of his native Wales, the work of such consistently high standard that it had quickly brought him recognition as one of the most gifted landscape painters of his generation.

Next morning it seemed at first as though Bran's plans for an outing were doomed to disappointment. When Naomi arrived in the kitchen for breakfast the room was in a rare state of chaos, with no sign of Megan.

Wondering what was wrong, Naomi filled a kettle and cut slices of bread to put in the toaster, then began clearing away, much to Megan's distress when that lady rushed in shortly afterwards.

'You mustn't do that, love!' she remonstrated.

'Why not?' Naomi carried on serenely. 'Something wrong, Megan?'

'It's Tal. He's not well, touch of flu, I think. He's ever so cross with me because I rang the doctor!'

'The best thing you could do. Here, sit down. I've just made some tea.'

'I can't sit down, Naomi, there's Bran's breakfast to see to yet——'

'Not for a moment,' said Naomi, pressing Megan into a chair. 'Just tell me how I can help.'

'You're helping already!' Megan subsided gratefully. 'I get so worried about Tal. He's got this bad chest. He's got dust too, like Bran's dad, only not so bad, mind. When he catches cold he gets this terrible cough.' She glanced at the clock and shot to her feet. '*Duw*, that's never the time? Bran must be wondering what's happened——'

'You tell me what to give him and I'll take him a tray,' said Naomi firmly.

'I can't let you do that!'

'Megan, calm down. Of course I can. I'm not working today, Look, while I eat this toast you make Bran's breakfast then I'll pop it along to his studio while you go back and see to Tal.'

Only Megan's worry over her husband persuaded her to let Naomi take Bran's breakfast-tray along to the studio. Naomi knocked on one of the double doors at the end of the corridor, then opened it carefully and backed into the studio, balancing the tray.

'Tal?' called Bran from the floor above. 'You're late. Is anything wrong —— ?' He stopped as Naomi began mounting the spiral stair. 'Hallelujah, unless Tal has taken to using perfume, I do believe it's you, Naomi.'

'Full marks,' panted Naomi as she reached the gallery bedroom. She put the tray down on the rather large table beside the bed, alongside the radio Bran had switched off at her approach. She eyed him closely to gauge his mood. He was sitting up in bed, propped against pillows, his chin dark with overnight stubble and his chest bare above the quilt.

'Please don't think I'm unappreciative,' said Bran, looking astonished, 'but why are you deputising for Tal this morning?'

'He's ill —— '

'Ill?' said Bran sharply. 'What's the matter?'

'Megan thinks it's flu, but what she's really worried about is his chest.'

'If you'd ever heard him cough you'd know why,' he said grimly. 'Tell her to call the doctor right away.'

'She's already done so.' Naomi hesitated. 'Megan's made you an omelette. Shall I cut it up a bit?'

'No, thanks. If you put the plate on my lap and hand

me a knife and fork I can manage. Just butter some toast and pour the coffee,' he instructed, and cursed under his breath. 'This puts the skids under our day out, blast it.'

Naomi added sugar to his coffee, stirring briskly. 'Not necessarily.'

He frowned. 'What do you mean?'

'If you weren't planning on going very far—or very fast—I could drive. As long as you'll put up with my Mini. I'm safer with the devil I know when it comes to cars.'

Bran chewed on some toast thoughtfully. 'You mean that?'

'I wouldn't have offered if I didn't,' she said with asperity. 'Look, if you're willing to trust yourself to my driving and my car we could leave Megan in peace to look after Tal—and I'll still get my outing.'

'Oh, in that case,' he said, grinning, 'I accept, with thanks.' He waited a moment. 'What's the matter?'

Something about an unshaven Bran, a smile gleaming in his remarkable eyes, was creating the now familiar havoc with Naomi's nervous system. Keeping her voice as businesslike as possible, she asked him if he needed any help with getting dressed.

'Why? Are you offering to wash my back?'

Naomi blushed fierily. 'Certainly not,' she snapped. 'I thought I could help you choose what you want to wear, that's all.'

He waved a hand in the direction of the bathroom. 'Thanks just the same, but Tal puts everything ready the night before in there. Sometimes I'm up and showered and dressed long before he gets here. Other times I laze around in bed until breakfast-time. It all depends on the mood I'm in.'

'I see.' Naomi took his plate and handed him a cup of coffee. 'Is the mood good or bad today?'

'Good, of course — can't you tell? The prospect of a day out in charming company like yours, Naomi, made the world seem bright this morning the moment I woke up.'

'Very flowery,' she said acidly. 'I'll leave you to drink your coffee and take the rest of the things down, then.'

'What time would you like to leave? It's sunny today, isn't it?'

'Yes. So far.' She thought for a moment. 'Give me a couple of hours, in case I can do anything for Megan before we go. Will that do?'

'Whatever you say; I'm in your hands. A happy thought!' he added, leering in her direction.

Naomi preserved a dignified silence as she went carefully down the spiral stair, amazed that Bran was too stubborn to use one of the other bedrooms in the house in the circumstances. In her opinion he was mad to insist on risking his neck on a stairway she found it hard enough to negotiate with two good eyes to see her way.

Megan was delighted to hear that Naomi had volunteered for the role of chauffeur.

'It was a lucky day for us when you came to work here,' she said fervently, fortunately too preoccupied with preparing a picnic lunch to notice the sudden shadow on Naomi's face.

The sun was shining with surprising warmth when Bran lowered himself carefully into Naomi's Mini. He looked relaxed, and even more attractive than usual to Naomi's eyes in an old suede jacket and yellow cashmere turtleneck, with a rather transatlantic air to his shining loafers and pale chinos.

'Where shall we go?' he asked, as Naomi got in beside him.

'If you don't mind I'd rather not venture too far

afield. My only view of this beautiful valley of yours was on the drive here the day I arrived. I'd like to explore it more fully.'

'Fine by me.' He turned his head towards her. 'Will you do something for me, Naomi?'

'If I can,' she said guardedly.

'All I want is a description from you as we drive. You can't drive fast along these roads, anyway, so you won't find it difficult.'

'But surely you know the Vale of Ewyas like the back of your hand!'

'True. But I'd like to see it through eyes new to it, like yours.'

It seemed little enough to ask. 'Fine,' she said, switching on the ignition. 'But in that case we're not likely to get very far. I don't drive fast at the best of times, but if I'm doing a commentary at the same time we'll be doing hours per mile instead of the other way round.'

He laughed and leaned back in his seat. 'Who cares when the air coming through the window is warm and spring-scented, and my guide has such a beguiling voice?'

'Which I'll be obliged to raise to shouting point if I'm to make myself heard if we pass any lambing sheds! Are your Welsh sheep a particularly noisy breed?'

'They probably like the sound of their own voices, like me and every other Welshman ever born.'

Naomi laughed. 'You said that, remember, not me!'

As she drove carefully down the steep, winding drive she felt a sudden lift of spirits. Today she would forget her guilt and her motive for coming to Gwal-y-Ddraig and the land of the Black Mountains. This was an outing, a pleasure trip, with a complex, attractive man for company, and sunshine to add the gilding on the gingerbread.

'There were showers early this morning,' she began, 'and I think there may be a few more lurking ahead, because directly over us there's a rainbow. It looks like a gleaming striped bridge spanning two of these amazing rounded mountain tops, with a thundery grey cloud beyond, a washed powder-blue sky above, and bright, wet green fields below.'

Bran nodded in appreciation. 'That's what I want to hear. Tal's a great driver and the best of men, but his description tends towards the terse.'

'I may run out of adjectives,' she warned.

'Before you do, tell me what you're wearing today.'

'You haven't asked me that for a while now.'

'Because every morning it was blue jeans, a shirt and sweater, and I could picture that much for myself. Is there any change today?'

'Oh, yes. It's my day off. I'm wearing navy leggings, a striped navy and white shirt and a thick, baggy red sweater. Bright red like a pillarbox. And today I've tied my hair back with a red ribbon, and I'm wearing shoes like yours, only navy blue leather instead of that lovely glossy chestnut shade.' She looked sideways at him curiously. 'Why the sigh?'

He shrugged, his mouth twisting in the way she'd come to know so well. 'I was just wishing I could see the face that goes with the clothes. The rest of you I can picture clearly enough, but not the face. It's bloody frustrating.'

'You're not missing much!'

'Stop putting yourself down! From my one respectful exploration I know there's nothing untoward about your face.'

'If you mean I don't have a nose like Concorde and

teeth like Bugs Bunny, you're right. I'm just not—pretty.'

'One day I'll find out for myself!'

Not, thought Naomi, if she could possibly help it. By the time Bran Llewellyn could see again, *if* he ever regained his sight, she would be back in London well out of his reach. In the meantime her task was to paint a picture for Bran. There was no lack of subject matter for description. Every bend in the road brought them to a different scene, each one as worthy of Bran's brush as the last.

After consulting with Bran Naomi eventually took the turning to Llanthony Priory, and parked the Mini in the small car park beyond the small, ancient church of St David.

'I won't get out,' said Bran quickly. 'You go ahead and explore. You can report on your findings when you get back. I've been here scores of times, so don't feel guilty. Is there a radio in your car?'

Naomi switched it on for him, left him with a Schubert symphony and hurried off to inspect the ruined priory. A tablet on one of the walls informed her she was on the site of the first Augustine foundation in Wales, and it was beautiful, even in its ruined state, with redstone arches graceful above a sward as green and smooth as a billiard table. Naomi cast a longing look at the small hotel cum pub built over what had once been the abbot's house. She would have liked to linger over coffee or a drink there with Bran, and felt a sudden sharp pang of sympathy with him for some of the simple pleasures in life he was missing.

Reluctant to leave him alone for long, she took a quick look round the tiny church of St David, impressed to find there had been a place of worship there since the sixth century, then on impulse she knelt and said a prayer before rejoining Bran.

'Well?' he asked. 'Were you pleased with what you found?'

'Who wouldn't be?' Naomi slid in beside him and leaned over to switch off the radio. She tensed as his long hand shot out to capture her wrist. 'What's the matter?'

'Several things. Your perfume, for one. It gave me a sudden urge to touch,' he said harshly, and released her.

Naomi subsided in her seat, heart thudding. 'Shall I drive on?'

'What time is it?'

'Just after twelve.'

He fumbled for the seatbelt. 'Where's the blasted socket for this thing?'

'Here.' Naomi leaned across and clipped the belt into place, her throat constricting as she sensed the tension in his body. 'Where shall we go now?'

He sighed explosively. 'I'd like to take you to a pub for lunch, but my face is too well known around here.'

'Oh, don't worry about lunch,' she said, deliberately cheerful as she started the car. 'I've got that organised — with Megan's help, of course. I'm going to drive back down the road until I find a spot where I can park the car again, and then we're going to have a picnic.'

CHAPTER FIVE

ACTING on instructions given earlier by Megan, Naomi rejoined the road through the valley and headed north along twists and bends which, Bran informed her, would bring them to the little whitewashed church of Capel-y-ffin if they went far enough.

Long before that point Naomi made for a turning and a farm gate where she could tuck the Mini out of harm's way. She undid her seatbelt and scanned the sky, but there was no sign of the earlier showers. 'It's quite warm,' she told Bran. 'I've brought a rug, and there's a rather inviting log out there. Would you like to sit outside in the sun? Or would you rather stay in here?'

'Is there anyone around?'

'Not a soul in sight.'

'Then lunch al fresco it is.'

Naomi jumped out of the car and went round to open the passenger door. Bran disdained her assistance until he was standing outside, but took her hand to gain the safety of the fallen tree-trunk. Naomi stooped inside the car for the rug, spread it on their impromptu couch, then lugged the picnic basket out on to the grass.

'How efficient you are,' remarked Bran from his perch. 'I feel loweringly superfluous.'

'Not at all,' contradicted Naomi cheerfully. 'You provide the company. No picnic worth its name is good if eaten on one's own.' She passed him a napkin and a plastic plate. 'What do you fancy?'

'If I told you it's ten to one you'd drive off and leave me here, at the mercy of passing strangers!'

Naomi glared at him, then laughed reluctantly. Icy glances of disapproval were pretty useless under the circumstances. She explained why she was laughing, then cast an eye over the contents of the basket.

'Megan's made sandwiches with some of the Wye salmon intended for your lunch at home, or you can have small crusty rolls filled with either liver pâté or the mustard-glazed ham we had roasted for dinner last night.'

'Lucullus himself couldn't ask for more,' declared Bran. 'I'll have something of everything, please, but only one thing at a time.'

Naomi was careful to anticipate Bran's every want as they made inroads on the picnic basket, listening raptly as he regaled her with snippets of local legend while they ate. To make up for not taking her to the nearby Skirrid Inn for lunch Bran told her something of its history instead, how the first recorded existence of the inn known as the Skirrid had been as early as fifty years after the Norman Conquest, when two brothers by the name of Crowther had been sentenced, James to nine months for robberies with violence, John to death by hanging from a beam in the inn for sheep stealing.

'In those days,' said Bran, deepening his voice deliberately, 'they believed the devil rode abroad, and the innkeeper kept a pot of "devil's brew" on the shelf above the fireplace, which gave rise to the saying "sip with the devil". And when the last of the customers had gone for the night a jug of *pwcca* was left on the inn doorstep to appease the spirits of darkness.'

'*Pwcca*?' queried Naomi, trying to get her tongue round the unfamiliar sound.

Bran spelt it for her. 'Shakespeare is rumoured to

have taken his idea for Puck of *Midsummer Night's Dream* from *y pwcca*.'

Naomi laughed. 'You Welsh take the credit for everything! And seem pretty preoccupied with the devil in these parts, too, by the sound of it.'

Bran gave her an enigmatic smile. 'The dragon, you may care to know, was believed to be a manifestation of the devil.'

Naomi shivered. 'So your house could just as well be called "Lair of the Devil", then.'

He grinned. 'I bet if you'd known that you'd have thought twice before setting foot in it, timorous Saxon!'

Sensibly, Megan had provided nothing more demanding for pudding from Bran's point of view than crisp green apples, and they munched in unison, until Naomi giggled suddenly and told Bran they bore a definite resemblance to the sheep grazing on the steep fields all round them.

'Do that again!' commanded Bran.

'Do what?'

'Giggle like a little girl.'

'Yuck! That sounds horrible — arch and coquettish.'

Bran shook his head. 'I can't see your face, Naomi. Yet. But I'm damn sure arch is the last word for you.'

'For which many thanks! Coffee?'

'No champagne?' he said, mock-aggrieved.

'Certainly not.' Naomi took his plate and napkin, but as she poured steaming coffee into beakers from a Thermos jug Bran turned to her suddenly and knocked the jug from her hand. Scalding coffee cascaded down Naomi's front, and she screamed involuntarily as the heat of the liquid penetrated right through the thick wool sweater and the shirt beneath.

'What is it?' demanded Bran wildly, stretching his hands towards her. But before he could make contact with her he tripped over a tree root and lost his balance. He grabbed at her instinctively and fell, taking her with him, swearing violently as he collapsed with her into an awkward heap on the grass behind the log. '*Naomi*,' he howled. 'Hell, what a clumsy swine I am. Are you all right?'

'A bit winded, but otherwise in one piece,' she said breathlessly, pinned by the muscular body sprawled awkwardly on top of her. 'Are *you* all right?'

He swore again under his breath. 'Not counting my dignity, yes.'

She waited, breathing unevenly, but he made no move to let her up. 'Do you need help to get on your feet, Bran? If you move over a bit I can ——'

'I *can* get up, but I seem to have lost the will to do so.' Bran shifted slightly, easing his weight a little, but making no other move to let her go.

Colour rushed to her face. 'Bran—please!'

But Bran wasn't listening. Eyes closed, he slid his hands over her blazing cheeks, then thrust them into her hair and bent his head, his mouth searching over her cheek until it found hers. At the touch of his lips Naomi gasped involuntarily, her lips parting beneath his. Bran groaned, his kiss suddenly fierce and voracious. He shifted until he was directly above her, his arms encircling her like manacles as he kissed her over and over again until her senses reeled. He muttered something, the words muffled against her mouth as he freed a hand so that he could trace the outline of her jaw, moving his fingers down her throat and lower to caress her breasts. And encountered sodden wool still hot to the touch. He flinched away from her with a curse.

'Naomi, you're soaked! The blasted coffee must have burnt like hell—why didn't you say, you little fool?' he demanded hoarsely.

She drew in a deep, shaky breath. 'I — I'm not scalded, my sweater's too thick.'

'Is that the truth?'

'Yes.'

'Let me touch you,' he demanded, reaching for her, but she intercepted his hands and scrambled ungracefully to her feet.

'I'm fine. Really.' She made a valiant effort to pull herself together. 'If you reach out in front you'll be able to steady yourself on the log. Or would you like me to help you up?'

'No, I bloody well wouldn't,' he said with sudden savagery, and hauled himself to his feet, staggering a little as he stood upright. 'Just get me back to the car.'

In taut silence Naomi guided him to the Mini, then left him to settle himself into the seat. Swiftly she gathered up the detritus of their lunch and packed it away in the basket, then tipped back the front seat and stowed everything into the back of the car.

'I suppose you expect an apology,' he said bitterly, fighting to jam his seatbelt into the socket without her help.

'Of course I don't. It — just happened.' She got in beside him, determined to lighten the atmosphere. 'I've learnt one thing today, though. Whoever said "easy as falling off a log" hadn't a clue what they were talking about.'

'Spare me the bright chatter,' he said through his teeth. 'Let's get home so you can get your clothes off.' He ground his teeth audibly. 'I mean —— '

'I know what you mean!' Red-cheeked, Naomi drove off down the winding road at uncharacteristically reckless speed, too distraught to be cautious for once. Even so it seemed hours before they reached Gwal-y-Ddraig, by which time the silence in the car was so intense she was ready to scream.

As they reached the house Megan emerged from the front door, her smile fading at the sight of Bran's grim, set face.

'Whatever's happened?' she asked sharply.

'Naomi can tell you,' snapped Bran, his mouth tightening as he was forced to accept her helping hand to get out of the car. 'I'm off to the studio.' He paused, suddenly remorseful. '*Sorry*, I forgot. How's Tal?'

'Only a cold, after all, the doctor said. Nothing a few hot drinks and a day's rest won't cure,' she assured him, and made to lead Bran indoors.

'I'll be all *right*. See to Naomi. I threw boiling water over her.' Bran shook off her hand and marched into the house, narrowly missing contact with the open door.

Megan flew to help Naomi, who was busy unloading the car. 'Never mind that, *bach*. Good gracious, just look at your jumper — come inside and take it off at once.'

Meekly Naomi let herself be fussed over, submitting to having her sweater and shirt stripped off in the kitchen, wincing as she heard Bran slam the studio doors shut behind him.

'My bra will probably never pass the whiteness test again,' said Naomi ruefully, looking down at herself. 'But I'm not burnt. My front's a tasteful shade of shrimp-pink, that's all. My sweater was thick enough to insulate me from the worst.'

'What a thing to happen,' said Megan, handing Naomi a towel. 'There, wrap yourself in that. I don't think you'll blister. I'll swill these things out for you before the stain sets.'

'Thank you, Megan.' Naomi swathed herself obediently then slumped down at the kitchen table. 'It was such a shame. Up to then we'd been having a really pleasant time.' She explained how the accident happened, but made no mention of the kisses. Those, she thought miserably, were best forgotten. By all concerned.

It took Naomi every last scrap of determination she possessed to go downstairs later that evening for dinner, only to be informed by Megan that Bran had refused anything to eat, and was barricaded in his studio. And since she was determined to keep Tal in bed for the day Megan suggested diffidently that Naomi might like to have her meal in the kitchen to keep her company.

'I would indeed,' said Naomi, secretly limp with relief.

'Bran's in a terrible mood tonight,' confided Megan, laying two places at the kitchen table.

Naomi, who knew precisely why, refrained from explaining. She felt that poor Megan had enough on her plate, without worrying because her beloved Bran was subject to the very normal frustrations of a man deprived of the sexual attentions he was used to. 'He'll be fine tomorrow,' she said cheerfully, and changed the subject.

Next morning Naomi woke early, and lay wondering what to do with her day off. From several points of view it seemed wise to take herself off out of the way for most of it. By the time she returned Bran might be back to normal. Although the black mood could well *be* normal for him for all she knew, she reminded herself. Yet he'd been the perfect companion yesterday until he'd begun to make love to her. Familiar heat enveloped her at the mere thought of it, and with a shiver she slid from the bed and went to stand at one of the windows, closing her mind to Bran's expert, hungry kisses as she gazed out on a day bright with sunshine. She would go out, she decided. If she was on stop until Bran gave her another tape she might just as well remove herself from his vicinity for a few hours and widen her knowledge of the hauntingly beautiful Welsh Marches.

'You're up and about early,' said Megan, when Naomi arrived in the kitchen. 'I thought you'd be having a nice lie-in.'

'Something I bet you don't indulge in very often, Megan,' said Naomi, smiling. 'The sunshine woke me early so I thought I'd take myself out for the day to do some more sightseeing. How's Tal?'

'Better this morning.' Megan's mouth tightened. 'Which is more than I can say for Bran. Like a bear with a sore head, he is.'

Naomi pulled a face. 'Still in a bad mood, then.'

'He gets moods, mind. Nothing to do with the blindness; he always did. What Welshman doesn't?' Megan laughed comfortably. 'Anyway, you eat your breakfast and I'll make you a nice picnic lunch.'

'You won't!' Naomi waved Megan to a chair. 'Come and have something with me, then I'll make my own picnic lunch, if you'll let me forage for myself.'

Megan subsided with a grateful sigh, and poured tea for them both. 'You take whatever you want, *bach*. And make sure you take plenty, mind, because it's only cold supper tonight. Tal's brother's coming to visit him this evening, so I'll leave you to see to Bran — that's if you don't mind,' she added anxiously.

Naomi, quailing secretly at the prospect, lied convincingly as she assured Megan she'd be glad to help out. Confronted with the prospect of a meal *à deux* with Bran later that evening, she found she badly needed a few hours away from the house and its owner; time to herself to get things in perspective.

All fingers and thumbs in her haste, Naomi packed her picnic in the Mini as quickly as she could, wrestling afterwards with the passenger door, which as usual was maddeningly difficult to close. At last she banged it shut impatiently, then looked up in dismay to see Bran approaching, his head raised at the familiar, questioning angle.

'Naomi?' he said peremptorily. 'Is that you?'

For a moment she contemplated diving into the car and taking off without talking to him, but common sense prevailed. Reluctantly she stayed put, her spirits plummeting at the grim set to his face. Bran Llewellyn's sightless, spectacular eyes were bloodshot and black-ringed as they turned in her direction.

'Were you just going to drive off without saying anything?' he demanded tersely.

'I didn't think you'd want to be disturbed.'

His face set in familiar, bitter lines. 'You mean it was just easier to take off without a word!'

'I didn't realise I had to clock in and out,' she cut back at him, suddenly out of patience. 'Do forgive me, Mr Llewellyn. I shall be out for a while, as it's Sunday and you've no work for me to do. I'm not sure how long, but if it's of any interest to you Megan's provided me with a picnic lunch, and unless I get hopelessly lost I'll be back in time for supper.'

He looked so thoroughly taken aback that Naomi's anger evaporated.

'My mistake,' he muttered dourly. 'I thought you were leaving for good.'

She sniffed. 'How could I? The job isn't finished yet.'

'I thought my sudden resort to basic male instincts had frightened you off.' He gritted his teeth. 'Is it any use saying I'm glad I was mistaken?'

'Yes. It is. Not,' added Naomi, 'that I'm idiot enough to turn tail and run over what happened yesterday.'

'I stand corrected,' he said sardonically. 'Tell me, *did* the coffee harm you?'

'No. My sweater is the heavy, oiled wool type — practically waterproof.' Naomi moved close enough to touch his hand with hers. 'It was just an accident, nothing to get het up about.'

'Unlike the lovemaking, which was no accident, and something I, at least, got very het up about,' he said, training his heavy tourmaline eyes on her with such accuracy that Naomi tensed.

'Something the matter?' he demanded.

'No. It's just that sometimes it's so hard to believe you can't see,' she said, her heart thumping.

His mouth twisted bitterly. 'While I, at the risk of sounding mawkish, find it bloody impossible to get used to it.'

'Yes,' she said, with sympathy. 'And since you've brought the subject up it's as good a time as any to say I quite understand.'

His brows flew together. 'Understand what?'

'Your reasons.'

'My reasons for what?'

'You know perfectly well what I mean,' she said tartly. 'Your reasons for — well, for making love to me.'

He raised a derisive eyebrow. 'I made love to you, Naomi, for one reason only. When I fell on top of you I went berserk. I could no more resist what followed than any other man in the same situation.'

'Oh.' Naomi swallowed, retreating a little. 'Well, I — I suppose it's quite natural, in the circumstances.'

Bran scowled. 'Circumstances?'

Naomi hesitated, trying to phrase it as tactfully as possible. 'The fact that you've had no contact with a woman for a while. I can understand you must be missing. . .' She trailed into silence at his expression.

'The love of a bad woman?' he enquired silkily.

'I was going to say feminine companionship,' she retorted, her colour high.

'But you've been providing that ever since you arrived, Naomi.' He smiled mirthlessly. 'What you really mean is that I've missed having someone to share my bed and slake my evil lust.'

'I wouldn't have put it quite like that,' she said huffily. 'But yes, that's more or less what I meant — perfectly understandable for a man like you.'

He folded his arms across his chest. 'What the hell do you mean by that?'

'Nothing derogatory. I meant you're obviously not the type of man used to sexual frustration.'

'If you believe that, I'm surprised you're not making your escape from the lair of the dragon right now, as fast as that old banger will take you, Naomi Barry!'

'Only when I've finished the work I came here to do,' she repeated, unruffled.

'Are you afraid a sharp exit might forfeit you the all-important money?'

Naomi, wanting badly to slap his face, ignored him. 'Time I was off, I think.'

'Naomi, wait. That was uncalled-for,' said Bran wearily. 'I've no right to inflict my bloody awful moods on you.'

Naomi's resentment lessened slightly. 'No, you haven't. But I don't mind. Well, not much, anyway.'

He laughed softly and put out a peremptory hand. 'Barring my mother and Megan, you're the only woman I've ever met who's so scrupulously truthful. Shall we shake and be friends?'

Praying he'd never discover how mistaken he was, Naomi put her hand gingerly into his. Bran squeezed it very gently.

'Off you go, then. And take note of what you see. I shall expect a full report over supper tonight.'

'Of course.' She hesitated. 'Perhaps you'd like me to read from the Sunday papers afterwards?'

He raised his eyebrows. 'What a magnanimous little soul you are, Naomi. I'd like that very much, as it happens. No doubt you've been informed that tonight we get pot luck. To give Megan a break I told her to leave a tray of bits and pieces in the studio for us.'

Naomi, not at all sure she cared for the hint of intimacy in the arrangement, couldn't steel herself to ask for a different venue for the meal. For one thing it sounded a lot easier for Megan. 'I'll see you later then.'

Naomi drove away from the house, feeling relieved that things were back to something approaching normal with Bran Llewellyn. As she negotiated the winding road down to the valley she frowned, trying to analyse what, exactly, *was* normal with Bran. Sometimes it was impossible to remember that she hadn't known him for years. She no longer thought of him as a famous artist. His blindness had cut through the usual formalities, and put them on a footing they would never have established under normal circumstances. Something she couldn't help feeling grateful for. It was new and oddly moving to have such a man dependent on her, because it was very obvious that Bran Llewellyn was a man normally dependent on no one — unless it was Tal and Megan.

Naomi drove slowly along the winding road, noting that bluebells were coming into flower to replace the departing daffodils. Her mouth drooped. By the time the bluebells were gone she'd be gone, too. Which would be a good thing. Her best course was to get the job over with and get the necessary information back to Diana as quickly as possible. But she'd be sorry to leave Gwal-y-Ddraig. She'd become very fond of Megan, Tal too. But the biggest wrench, she knew perfectly well, would be parting from Bran.

Her cheeks warmed as she remembered her own response to his kisses, how ravished she'd been by his urgency as his arms practically cracked her ribs. She sighed. Her sudden propulsion into Bran's arms might well have sent him momentarily berserk, as he said. She had all the curves and hollows of any normal female. But if he could have seen her as well it would never have happened. Naomi smiled bitterly. But if he'd been able to see there'd have been no fall and the incident would never have happened. Which, from her own point of view, would have been by far the best thing. Bran Llewellyn's lovemaking, brief though it had been, came into the unforgettable category.

As Naomi turned off on the sunlit, deserted road to Skenfrith she put Bran's kisses from her mind to pay full homage to the scenery. The rolling, rounded hills of this part of the Marches, so near to the Black Mountains of Llanthony, were subtly different in their green, inviting allure. It was hard to believe that once blood had been shed so copiously among these hills when the Normans fought to subdue the Welsh as they forced their harsh imprint on the border country.

Naomi made first for Whitecastle, the first of the Trilateral, the three castles which had once formed the main defence for the north-eastern corner of old Monmouthshire. Deeply impressed by the imposing, moated ruin, she took some photographs, then headed for Skenfrith, a few miles further on. She found little remained there of the original castle other than a ruined tower and some outer walls, but along with the mill and several beautiful houses it was built of the same rose-bronze sandstone as Gwal-y-Ddraig. Pierced by a sudden longing to share her delight in it all with Bran, she parked her car alongside the Bell Inn and walked through the tiny village to take a brief look at the castle before going on to the church, which possessed a tower topped by what looked remarkably like a dovecote, a form of church architecture Naomi had never seen before.

Inside the peaceful, welcoming St Brigid's she found the sixteenth-century tomb of one John Morgan and his family of Skenfrith, and in a glass case behind a curtain the Skenfrith Cope, an exquisite example of fifteenth-century embroidery on velvet, a miracle in its own right for having escaped destruction from two Cromwells, both Henry the Eighth's Thomas and the later Lord Protector himself. But the feature which impressed Naomi most of all was the impressive roll at the back of the church giving the names of the Lords of Skenfrith, among them William de Braose and John of Gaunt, Duke of Lancaster. Her eyes widened as she noted that the first on the list, one Bach, Son of Cadivor ap Gwaethvoed, Prince of Cardigan, pre-dated the Conquest by a year. What, she wondered, fascinated, had happened to Bach when the Norman Brientius de L'Isle had come on the scene in 1066?

It was so late by the time Naomi got back that she had to rush over her bath to get dressed in time for supper.

'You look as though you've had a good day, love,' commented Megan, as Naomi hurried into the kitchen.

'I did. What a beautiful part of the world you live in,' said Naomi fervently, as she hoisted the tray Megan had ready. 'I'll take this to the studio for you.'

'Can you manage? I've been spoilt today,' Megan declared, smiling. 'I had a nap this afternoon while Bran sat with Tal, and now you're fetching and carry-ing for me ——'

'I should think so. It's little enough to do. I'll come

back for the coffee tray in a minute.' Naomi smiled cajolingly. 'Only can I have a pot of tea, Megan?'

'You can have anything you like, love,' promised Megan fondly. '*Duw*, but I'll miss you when you leave.'

Naomi went off with the tray hurriedly, trying to outrun the guilt which had dogged her permanently since her arrival. In the studio she found Bran stretched out on the sofa, listening to a recording of Sir Geraint Evans as Dr Dulcamara in the first act of *L'Elisir d'Amore*. The dramatic, wonderfully resonant voice filled the room, full justice done to its timbre, not only by Bran's state-of-the-art equipment, but by the acoustics of the high-ceilinged studio. Lost to the world as he listened, for once Bran failed to hear Naomi come in until she put the tray down on a table near his sofa. He shot upright, pressing the off button on the remote control.

'Naomi? You're back.'

'Yes, indeed — but don't switch the music off on my account. I've got to go back for the coffee, anyway.'

'I should be fetching it myself,' he said morosely. 'I wish to God my eyes would start behaving themselves.'

'Perhaps you'll have good news from the consultant tomorrow,' she said briskly. 'By the way, how will you get to see him? Will Tal be fit enough to drive?'

'Megan says he is.' Bran smiled wryly. 'And, believe me, she wouldn't let Tal out of the house if she thought he wasn't up to it. I've salved my conscience by insisting she comes along too. Can you cope on your own until we get back?'

'I'm sure I can manage a sandwich and a pot of tea for myself. In fact,' she added, 'I'm perfectly willing to have a shot at dinner for us all as well, given the go-ahead.'

'I can just see Megan's face if I——' He halted, grimacing. 'Which I can, you know. In my mind.'

'I'm sure you can,' said Naomi cheerfully. 'She's a very memorable lady. I'll just dash back for the coffee-tray. Won't be a moment.'

'Has Tal's brother arrived?' Bran asked when she rejoined him.

'Not yet. He's coming after chapel, according to Megan.' Glad there was no reversion to the tension of their morning encounter, Naomi began an animated account of her day's travels as she helped Bran choose from the array of delicacies.

'That's better,' he said eventually, as he accepted some luscious fruitcake to round off the meal.

'The fruitcake?'

'No, you. I'm obviously forgiven.'

'Look, Bran,' she said bluntly, 'there was nothing to forgive. Really.'

His head swivelled towards her. 'Does that mean you wouldn't object if it happened again?'

'I draw the line at libations of boiling coffee,' she parried, her pulse racing.

'That, as you know perfectly well, was not what I meant,' he said impatiently. '*Would* you object, Naomi?'

'If you mean the kisses I probably wouldn't in practice,' she said with complete truth. 'You must have noticed I wasn't exactly fighting you off. But in theory, which is what I'll keep to, I do object. I came here to help with your autobiography, not console you for what you're missing out on sexually.'

Bran's eyebrows met his hair for an instant. '*Diawl*—you don't pull your punches, Naomi, do you?'

'I believe in making things clear! Coffee?'

'If that's the only thing on offer, yes.'

'It's not. I'm perfectly willing to read the Sunday

papers to you as well,' she said lightly, as she handed him his cup.

'What a saint you are, Naomi.'

Her mouth tightened. 'No way. Sanctity is the last thing I lay claim to. Talking of which, I saw the most wonderful church today.' And with an enthusiasm designed to divert Bran she described St Brigid's to him, delighted when she found he was familiar with all three places she'd visited.

The dovecote tower, he told her, had once fulfilled a very practical purpose when the Welsh border was subject to sudden raids, which was the reason for walls five feet thick, and its surmounting 'dovecote', which could house pigeons and provisions for eating, as well as bells.

'Did you notice the great timber bolt on the west door?' Bran asked.

'I did, indeed.' Naomi touched his hand in lieu of the smile he couldn't see. 'At Skenfrith it was so easy to picture how things once were, where everything was so close together with the church as its nucleus. Grosmont was beautiful, too, but there the castle was more detached, and looked more sophisticated, somehow. Probably that tall, elegant chimney on the bit added by John of Gaunt had something to do with it.'

'Nevertheless Grosmont was a busy town in medieval times, hence the very large church.' Bran grinned. 'Unfortunately a fellow Welshman of mine, Owain Glyndwr, torched the place in 1405 and it never really recovered.'

Naomi laughed. 'Violent lot, you Celts.'

The evening passed quickly as Naomi read excerpts from the newspapers, which led to discussions on various news items until Bran decided Naomi needed a rest and aimed his remote control at the stereo system so that they could listen to the rest of the first

act of *L'Elisir d'Amore*. When it was finished Bran
went over to remove the disc from the machine, his
fingers unerring as he replaced it in its case and
returned it to the row of compact discs on a shelf fixed
to the wall at the back of the alcove.

When Bran returned to the sofa Naomi laid a hand
on his.

'Now I *am* impressed.'

'At last!' He held on to her hand.

Naomi let it stay, reluctant to disturb the mood.
'How do you know which disc is where?'

'Simple. Tal arranged them for me in alphabetical
composer order, then together we numbered them off
and I memorised the numbers. When I want *Otello* I
simply count along the row until I find it.' He turned
his head towards her, smiling a little. 'Putting the disc
in the machine is relatively easy, of course. We inhabit
a push-button world.'

'Which you cope with so well——'

'No, I don't,' he said swiftly, his fingers tightening
on hers. 'You know exactly what a swine I can be at
times. If I were really coping I wouldn't give in to
these bloody awful moods.'

'Ah,' said Naomi slyly, 'but Megan tells me you've
always had those. Your present affliction is nothing to
do with it.'

'Megan,' said Bran forcefully, 'talks too much!'

'As far as I'm concerned,' warned Naomi, 'Megan
can do no wrong.'

'She feels the same about you,' said Bran drily.
'She'll miss you when you leave.' His voice dropped
half an octave. 'So will I.'

Naomi sat very still, her eyes bleak as she stared the
length of the big room at the portrait on the easel.
'Only for a while. The moment you can see again your
beautiful Allegra will come running back here.'

'I doubt it. She doesn't like Gwal-y-Ddraig. Too remote.' Eyes closed, Bran leaned his head against the velvet swathed across the back of the sofa. 'Allegra's an urban creature of nightclubs and theatres and endless lunches with girlfriends.'

'Where did you fit into all that?' asked Naomi curiously.

'I didn't. She posed for her portrait in my studio in London. Sometimes she'd coax me to take her to the theatre, or whatever restaurant was the latest craze among her set.'

'Do you still love her?'

'No. But then, I never did.' Bran stroked a long finger over the back of Naomi's hand. 'I was just hot to share her bed.' He turned his head and opened his eyes on hers so accurately that she tensed involuntarily. 'Something in your tone tells me you disapprove strongly of Allegra.'

'I don't know the lady—but I'd disapprove of anyone who behaved as she has.' Naomi scowled blackly at the portrait. 'If one loves someone it shouldn't make a scrap of difference if he's blind, injured, disfigured or—or anything else.'

Bran's eyebrows rose. 'Such passion, Naomi!'

She subsided, embarrassed. 'Sorry. I'll get off my soapbox.'

'Those were very heartfelt sentiments, Naomi. Were you speaking from experience?' he asked curiously.

'If you're asking if someone once left me for much the same reason, then the answer's yes.'

'But you've never been blind, surely?'

'No, of course not.' She tried, without success, to tug her hand away. 'My handicap was too trivial for words. I was just stupid enough to set up house with a man who said he loved me for my personality, my sense of humour, even my brain. Then he subjected me to a particularly public form of humiliation by leaving me for the new receptionist at the firm where we both worked. She's the cutest thing you ever saw: all errogenous zones and yards of hair. No brain. Probably no sense of humour. But not even Greg could expect everything—and I must be barking mad to tell you all this,' added Naomi shortly; 'enough to put anyone in a bad mood.'

'Of course it isn't,' he said impatiently. 'But I don't follow you. Where does a handicap come into this?'

'My looks, Mr Llewellyn! In the end it wasn't enough for Greg to have someone to love and laugh with. He wanted a beautiful face to look at as well.'

'Instead, you mean,' Bran snorted. 'By the sound of it you're well shot of the jerk.'

'That's what I said about Allegra,' Naomi reminded him. 'But you didn't agree, as I recall.'

'True. But since then I seem to have come round to your point of view.' His mouth curved in a sardonic smile. 'Perhaps we should introduce Allegra to your erstwhile swain. They'd make a great pair.'

Naomi forced a laugh. 'So they would. Sorry I sounded off like that. As a rule I find it impossible to discuss Greg at all.'

'Perhaps this is one time when my blindness is an advantage,' said Bran. 'The priest can't see the penitent in the confessional, remember.'

'You're nothing like my idea of a priest!'

'Good. In that case you won't be shocked.' And before Naomi realised what he meant she was in his arms and Bran's lips were testing the delicate skin beneath her eyes for tears before they moved lower to settle unerringly on her mouth.

CHAPTER SIX

NAOMI pushed fiercely at the arms encircling her, but Bran made nonsense of her struggles.

'Why not?' he demanded arrogantly.

'I gave you my reasons earlier on.'

'But I'm not trying to lure you to bed, Naomi.' He stifled her protests with a kiss so expert and victorious that she subsided against him, defeated, as his tongue caressed and invaded in a way which put paid to any last remaining shreds of resistance. It was a long time before he raised his head a little to move his cheek against hers. 'What harm is there in taking a little comfort from each other?' he said unevenly.

Naomi drew in a deep, shaky breath. 'Pure sophistry.'

'No. Plain common sense, *cariad*. Besides,' he added, laughing suddenly. 'Can you imagine the havoc if I tried to carry you up that staircase over there? I've only just mastered getting up there as a solo performance!'

Naomi giggled involuntarily, and made no further move to push him away. Sensing the change in her, Bran lifted her on his lap and leaned back in the corner of the sofa, cradling her against him.

'There, you see? Isn't that good?'

'I wouldn't have said good exactly — nor wise.'

'Miss Practical!'

'Not all the time, alas.'

Bran gave a deep sign of pleasure as he smoothed his cheek over her hair. 'This is very good for *me*, anyway, wise or not. And it's nothing to do with raging lust and this frustration you keep alluding to with such maidenly disapproval. I just want to touch. I *need* to touch, Naomi. The way I need to breathe and eat.'

'Does it make up a little for not being able to see?'

'Yes.' Bran moved his hand down over her temple and cheekbone. 'Though to match your honesty, Naomi, the blindness isn't my only reason for wanting to touch you.'

'I've told you before, you really wouldn't feel the same if you could see me.'

The hand moved to grasp her chin firmly. 'How can you possibly know that? I refuse to believe it. All right, so your self-esteem took a dive when this Greg of yours took off with someone else. But he's probably the type who can't stick to one woman anyway. I very much doubt it had anything to do with this face.' Bran's lips touched her forehead and moved down her nose and along her cheekbones until he reached her mouth, his lips gentle at first, then fierce as though he meant to underline his words. Naomi responded in kind, abandoning herself to the pleasure she discovered was mutual when Bran crushed her close against his thudding heartbeat.

'Maybe comfort wasn't quite the right word,' he panted. 'Perhaps we'd better stick to conversation after all. No, you don't!' He jerked Naomi back against him as she tried to sit up. 'I prefer to talk with you on my lap.'

'It's no aid to serious conversation,' she pointed out breathlessly.

'I disagree. I think it's the best possible way to hold a conversation. So let's talk about this man of yours.'

'No. Let's not.'

'All right.' Bran ran his fingers down her spine. 'Tell me, is this your sister's silk shirt again tonight?'

'No. This one's mine. Birthday present from my mother.'

'What colour is it?'

'Raspberry-red.'

'And the skirt?'

'Same one — black.'

'And short,' said Bran, his exploratory fingers finding her knee. She slapped them and he returned his hand to clasp the other one at her waist. 'Pax! Knees, I take it, are out of bounds.'

'You bet they are. Look, I really should go.' She tried to sit up but he tightened his grip. 'Bran, please, it's time I went to bed.'

'Not yet. Stay a little longer and tell me about this sister of yours. Does she look like you?'

'Not a bit,' said Naomi glumly. 'Diana's tall, red-haired and beautiful. You'd never know we were sisters.'

'And what does the beautiful Diana do for a living?' asked Bran curiously.

Naomi willed herself to stay relaxed. 'She works for a publisher.' Which was only a whiteish lie. The *Chronicle* was certainly published every day.

'And is she married?'

'No.'

'Too wrapped up in her career?'

'More or less.' Naomi freed herself determinedly and slid off his lap. 'I must take these things back to the kitchen.'

Bran rose to his feet carefully. 'I suppose it's useless to try and dissuade you.' He stood listening as she tidied the trays. 'But before you go, tell me something, Naomi.'

She stilled, her back to him. 'What do you want to know?'

'This man of yours. Did he stay with the queen of

the reception desk, or did he move on to pastures new?' Bran caught her by the hand and turned her towards him, alert to her urge to escape.

'I don't know,' Naomi drew in a deep breath. 'For ages I couldn't bear to hear his name. By the time I could it seemed pointless to make enquiries. By then I had a room-mate who'd never met him, and Diana's opinion of Greg discouraged any mention of him.'

'Try to find out,' advised Bran. 'I'd lay odds he's gone on to someone else by now, maybe more than one.'

'I doubt it. Susie was — is — a stunningly pretty girl.' Naomi paused, eyes narrowed. 'On the other hand, you've roused my curiosity. Maybe I will ask. Or get someone to do it for me.'

'Good girl.' Bran tugged on her hand, drawing her nearer. 'Stay, Naomi.'

'No — please, I must go.' Naomi pulled her hand away and seized the tray, rattling it ostentatiously, then blushed as his slow smile told her he knew exactly what she was about.

'Goodnight, then, Scheherazade.'

'Goodnight.' She hesitated. 'I hope all goes well tomorrow.'

'Say a little prayer for a miracle!'

Naomi was glad when the others had finally set off on their trip to Cardiff the following morning. Megan had been very uptight as Naomi ate her breakfast in the kitchen. Bran, it seemed, had sent his tray back virtually untouched, and when Naomi asked if she should pay a quick visit to the studio to wish him good luck Megan shook her head.

'I wouldn't, love. He's a bit tense. Can't blame him, mind, but if I were you I'd leave him be. He gave me two tapes to put on your desk, by the way.'

'Oh, right, I'll start work, then.' Naomi patted Megan on the shoulder. 'Chin up.'

Naomi found it hard to start work. She made a show of switching on the word processor and putting a tape in the cassette player, but it was hard to concentrate on Bran's voice for once. For the simple reason, she informed herself crossly, that the mere sound of it makes you want to run to put your arms round him and tell him everything will be all right.

She was on her feet and halfway across the room to do so when the door opened and she cannoned into Bran in the doorway.

He grasped her involuntarily, his fingers digging into her waist. 'Where are you off to in such a hurry?'

'I was coming to see you.'

'I gave Megan the tapes.'

'I know. I just—needed to see you.'

He pulled her against him, kissing her as though his life depended on it. 'And I needed that,' he muttered hoarsely as he let her go. 'A talisman against the day.'

Naomi grasped his hands hard. 'You won't need a talisman. Everything will be fine, I know it. What time will you be back?'

'Some time this afternoon.'

'I'll see you later, then.'

The grooves deepened alongside Bran's mouth. 'I wish I could say the same, Naomi.'

'You will see,' she said emphatically. 'Not today, maybe, but very definitely soon. I feel it in these famous bones of mine.'

'Bran!' called Megan, from the hall. 'Are you ready? Tal's in the car.'

'Coming.' Bran reached out a hand and Naomi put hers into it, grasping the long fingers.

'Good luck.'

Once everything was quiet Naomi settled down in

earnest to work, determined to finish both tapes before the day was over, and in the process keep her mind off what was happening in Cardiff. It was just a check-up, she assured herself. But despite her brave words to Bran she was afraid the consultant might give him bad news, tell him the condition was not temporary after all, that Bran must learn to live with his blindness for the rest of his life.

Naomi finished the first tape by noon, at which point it became obvious that only a little more work was necessary before the short, concise autobiography would be finished. She thrust the second tape into a drawer hastily, and went off to make tea. She drank it at the kitchen table, her eyes dark with depression at the thought of leaving Gwal-y-Ddraig—and Bran Llewellyn—in only a few days' time. Her spirits sank still lower as she went back through the hall to find a letter from Diana among the others left by the postman.

Diana, it seemed, had been afraid to trust her request to the telephone in case the conversation was overheard.

The thing is, Naomi, Craig took me out for a drink after work last night and I let slip about the article. He's really keen on the idea, so *please* post off anything you've got right away, love—about the house and lifestyle in his Welsh retreat, and so on.

Diana signed off with reiterated gratitude, love and kisses, leaving Naomi staring at the page in dismay.

She raced up to her room and grabbed the telephone to dial the *Chronicle*'s number.

'Diana?' she demanded when her sister came to the phone. 'It's me.'

'Naomi! I thought you couldn't talk——'

'Everyone's out. I must be quick before they get

back. Look, do I have to do this? You were the one who told me to come home!'

'I know, but since you hung on down there I assumed you'd come round to the idea, especially as it could do such a lot for me.' Diana sounded uptight. 'Jack Porter, Craig's deputy, is leaving on Friday. This story could be the decider as to whether I get the job or not.'

'Surely there's something else you could write about ——'

'Nothing that someone else isn't writing about as well on some other paper! You know perfectly well your man never gives interviews. I'll be very careful, I promise. You *know* I wouldn't write anything libellous. In any case this isn't gossip, it's just a feature —' Diana halted, sighing. 'But if you can't, you can't. I won't press you, love.'

'Oh, all right,' said Naomi unhappily. 'But for heaven's sake make sure the article's not out until I get back. I'd hate anyone to find out before I leave. Everyone's so kind here.'

'Including him?'

'As it happens, yes.' Naomi gritted her teeth. 'But don't worry, I'll do it. Just for you. I'll drive down to the main road and post whatever I have off to you now before everyone gets back.'

'Where's he gone?'

'Cardiff.'

'Why?'

'How should I know? I'm only the hired help.'

'If you send me this information you'll be more like fairy godmother as far as I'm concerned, and believe me, I appreciate it. I haven't forgotten the Bahamas.'

'I don't need a trip to the Bahamas. But you can do something else for me.'

'Anything!'

'Can you find out what Greg's doing these days — and who he's doing it with?'

As Diana promised, her name was called in the background, and she rang off hastily with more fervent thanks. Quickly, before she could change her mind, Naomi took her notes from the wardrobe, stuffed them in an envelope and addressed it to Diana at the *Chronicle*, then ran downstairs to drive down to the postbox on the main road. By the time she got back to the house afterwards an old, familiar pounding had started up in one side of her head, and she felt hideously sick.

Frantic with pain, Naomi knew of old that there was nothing she could do except take to her bed and stay there until the migraine released its grip. Crime and punishment, she thought in misery, as she lay in her darkened bedroom, unable to read, or listen to the radio or do anything at all other than let the waves of pain wash over her. At one stage she staggered to the bathroom and threw up, and felt better for a while. But the pain soon began gripping her head again with pincer-like contractions, rising to a crescendo which sent her to the bathroom for another bout of nausea that left her shivering and wretched as she crawled feebly back to bed.

She had no idea what time it was when she heard the car draw up outside below her window. Soon afterwards Megan came looking for her, eyeing the drawn curtains in alarm as she hurried over to the huddled figure in the bed. 'I've been looking everywhere for you, *bach*. Whatever's the matter? Is it a cold, like Tal?'

'No,' croaked Naomi, 'migraine.'

Megan clicked her tongue in sympathy. 'There's nasty. Do you get them often?'

'Now and then, but never mind me.' Naomi struggled upright, clutching her head. 'How's Bran?'

'The specialist was very pleased with him. He's confident it won't be long before Bran's sight returns.' Megan piled pillows behind Naomi and straightened the covers. 'Now just lie still, there's a good girl. *Duw*, you're a terrible colour. Aren't there some pills you can take?'

'No use while I'm throwing up.'

'You've been sick as well? Poor girl, let me make you some tea——'

'No! No, thank you, Megan.' Naomi tried to smile. 'Tell Bran I'm sorry I couldn't work this afternoon.'

Megan snorted. 'I should think not, indeed; you have a good rest! I'll leave you in peace and come up later.'

Much to Naomi's relief the pain began to lessen slowly after Megan's visit, taking the nausea with it, and eventually she slept. When she woke it was almost dark. She switched on the lamp then slid cautiously out of bed on legs which wobbled precariously as she made for the bathroom. After washing her face and brushing her teeth Naomi tidied her hair gingerly and staggered back to bed to lie against the stacked pillows, washed out, but blissfully free from pain except for a slight soreness about the head and a familiar floating feeling. The migraine, as she knew from bitter experience, was stress-related; a direct result of sending the notes to Diana.

A few minutes later Megan appeared. 'I've been up before,' she told Naomi, 'but you were out for the count. How do you feel, my lovely?'

'Much better, thank you, Megan.' Naomi could smile by this time. 'A bit weak and feeble, but no headache any more.'

'That's good. I'll fetch you something to eat.'

'Oh, Megan, not at this time of night. Some tea will be fine — and I can make that up here.'

Megan looked shocked. 'Certainly not! I made some chicken soup for Bran's starter tonight, so I'll bring you some of that and some nice crisp toast to go with it. You can't sleep on an empty stomach, now, can you?'

Naomi gave in meekly, surprised to find that now food had been mentioned she was a little hungry, and when Megan arrived with the meal it was no real effort to eat everything provided.

After Megan had gone Naomi switched on her portable radio and lay listening to some music, wondering disconsolately if Bran had missed her company at dinner. She felt furious with herself for getting ill — one whole day of Bran's company wasted, when there were so few days left. By the weekend, however much she tried to spin out the work, she'd have no more excuse to stay. She tried to read, but when her eyes protested she tossed the book away impatiently, and lay back against the pillows, feeling suddenly caged by the pretty, comfortable room. She wanted to be down in the studio with Bran, reading to him or just talking to him. Or lying in his arms on the sofa, said a brutally candid voice inside her head.

Naomi lay with eyes closed and fists clenched, trying to block the thought out. But shutting out the light threw Bran's face into sharper focus in her mind; the thick, sable eyelashes and translucent green eyes, his shock of crow-black hair and the sensuous, irresistible curve to his bottom lip. She sat up, and tried to arrange the pillows in greater comfort behind her sore head, then stilled as she heard a quiet knock at the door.

'Come in,' she said warily, assuring herself it was only Megan.

But the door opened to reveal the tall, unmistakable figure of Bran Llewellyn. She gazed wide-eyed, convinced for a moment that her fevered imagination had conjured him up to torment her, until the reality of his deep, confident voice as he said her name won a smile of such radiant welcome from her it was as well he couldn't see.

'Bran—please come in.' She leapt out of bed and flew across the room to take his hand. 'Careful, there's a little chair beside the door, and another near the bed where Megan was sitting. Come and sit down. Are you all right? Did the consultant really say there's an improvement? Were you tired after the trip——?'

'Hey!' he said, laughing, and felt for the chair. 'Let me get a word in, chatterbox. I'm fine, you're the invalid.'

'No, I'm not. I had a migraine, that's all.'

'Then close the door and get back into bed,' he ordered.

Naomi did as he said, touching his hand fleetingly as she passed him to get under the covers. 'I'm sorry I missed dinner.'

'It was lonely without you, Naomi.'

She relaxed against the pillows, content just to look at him. Early that morning he'd been dressed in a formal dark suit for his consultation, but tonight he was wearing a blue chambray shirt and crimson sweater, his long legs encased in navy corduroy.

'Why are you so quiet?' he asked softly.

'I was just looking at you. You look different, somehow.'

'It must be the glow of optimism, *cariad*.' His smile dazzled her. 'It seemed like tempting providence to mention it before, but for the past few days I've noticed a greater degree of sensitivity to light, and the consultant confirmed it. He says my sight should be fully restored before long.'

Naomi leaned over impulsively to clasp his hand. 'That's wonderful news, Bran—I'm so glad.'

His hand closed over hers. 'You really are, too, aren't you?'

'Of course I am,' she said indignantly. 'Why shouldn't I be?'

'Because then I'll be able to see this face of yours. Something I'm looking forward to, because I refuse to believe that voice could possibly come from a face I didn't want to look at.'

'It doesn't matter, anyway,' she said forlornly. 'Unless your sight returns by the weekend you'll never know. I'll have finished the draft of your book by then.'

Bran's hand tightened on hers. 'What has that to do with it? If I can see I can drive. So what's to stop me coming to visit you in London?'

Naomi went cold. It had never occurred to her that he might want to see her again, once she'd left Gwal-y-Ddraig.

'By the deadly silence,' said Bran cuttingly, 'I take it the idea doesn't appeal.'

'It—it isn't that.'

'Then what's the problem?'

'It's pretty obvious, really. At the moment I'm the only woman around, except for Megan,' she began, trying to be reasonable. 'It's very flattering to have you enjoy my company, of course, but at the same time I don't kid myself that once you're back to normal you'll feel the same. Think of all the other woman you'll have falling over each other to welcome you back once you're in circulation again.'

'What a pretty picture you paint of my sex life, Naomi,' he said mockingly, 'and don't pull away, I've no intention of letting you have your hand back just yet. In fact,' he said, his voice deepening, 'your migraine is the only thing keeping me from holding a great deal more of you than your hand.'

'Then for once I'm grateful to the migraine,' she said tartly.

'Why? Is the idea such a turn-off?' he demanded.

Naomi sighed impatiently. 'You know very well it's not. It must have been quite obvious, both last night and this morning, that I like being in your arms far more than I should — or is wise.'

Bran got to his feet, still holding her hand, then felt for the bed and sat down on the edge of it, close enough to touch his free hand to her face. 'Naomi, we're both single and over age. Why shouldn't we take advantage of something that gives us both such pleasure?'

'You know perfectly well why,' she said irritably, trying to shrink into the pillows. 'I've got another life to return to next week, and I want to get back to it all in one piece, Bran Llewellyn.'

'"The lady",' said Bran very softly, '"doth protest too much, methinks".' And he bent close to kiss her, but when she turned her cheek to his seeking mouth he stiffened and got to his feet, breathing in deeply. 'All right, Naomi. I'll leave you to your chaste and lonely bed, and I'll go back to mine. Reluctant and unwilling, but I'll go.'

'Let me see you to the door,' she said quickly, sliding from the bed to take his hand.

'You don't make it any easier,' he said harshly, as she led him across the room. 'I may not be able to see you, but I can feel your pulse throbbing under my fingers, smell perfume and warm, flustered female. It's driving me crazy!' He stopped dead, tugging sharply on her hand so that she fell against him, and this time when he bent his head his mouth fastened unerringly on hers.

Naomi gave up. She slid her arms around him and held him close, her breasts hard and urgent against his chest through the thin cotton of her nightgown. He muttered something unintelligible against her mouth, then kissed her with a growling, starving insistence she responded to with such fervour that they were both breathing in agonised gasps when Bran tore his mouth from hers at last. He held her away a little to run his hand over her face and down her throat to the upper curves of her breasts, and Naomi's blood pounded in her ears, her eyes glazed as she stared up into the intent, passionate face above her. A great shiver ran through her as he slid the nightgown from her shoulders and cupped a breast in each hand, then bent his head to take each hardening nipple in his mouth in turn.

Naomi uttered a smothered, hoarse cry and clutched wildly at him for support, then Bran suddenly raised his head, listening.

'*Hell*, no—' He gave her an ungentle push. 'Back to bed. At the double.'

Naomi tugged at her nightgown and dived across the room to the bed. She pulled the covers up to her throat as Bran made for the door, thrusting his hand through his hair. As he reached it someone knocked quietly, and Bran took a deep breath, squared his shoulders then opened the door, smiling wryly.

'Hello, Megan.'

Megan, in a flowered dressing-gown with her hair neatly pinned beneath a bright pink hairnet, looked thunderstruck. 'Bran? What in the world are you doing here?'

'I came to ask after the invalid,' he said, with a composure much envied by Naomi.

Megan took his arm and made him sit down on the chair by the door. 'Just you wait there a minute, Bran Llewellyn. Before I go to my bed I'd like you safely back in the studio, if you don't mind.' She crossed the room to look at Naomi, frowning as she saw hectic colour in cheeks which had been ashen earlier on. 'Are you all right, love? You've got a temperature by the look of you.' She laid a hand on Naomi's forehead and clicked her tongue at its heat.

'I'm fine,' said Naomi, glad for once that Bran had no way of catching her eye. 'My headache's gone and I'll be fighting fit in the morning, I promise.'

'I hope so,' said Megan doubtfully, and glanced across at Bran, whose face was so rigidly expressionless that Naomi knew he was desperate to laugh. 'I just thought I'd come and see if Naomi wanted anything before I go to bed. Never thought I'd see you here, Bran.'

'I, too, wanted to see how Naomi was faring. Great minds think alike, Megan, *bach*.' He got to his feet and held out a hand in the direction of her voice. 'But I'll go quietly. Take me, I'm yours!'

'You just stop your old nonsense!' Megan laughed, shaking her head as she turned back to Naomi. 'And you get a good night's sleep, my girl. Goodnight.'

'Goodnight, Megan. Thank you for coming.' Naomi swallowed a laugh as Bran turned his face towards her with a bland, innocent smile.

'You haven't thanked *me* for coming, Naomi.'

'And thank you, too. You're all very kind.' Her eyes danced as she smiled and Megan sighed.

'There's a pity you can't see her, Bran. She's got a lovely smile.'

'Really? According to Naomi she's as ugly as sin.'

Naomi could have hit him as Megan stared at her in astonishment.

'Why ever did you tell him that?'

'I didn't say that, exactly!'

'I should hope not.' Megan crossed to Bran and took him by the arm. 'Naomi's got a dear little face, believe me.'

'Oh, I do,' Bran assured her. 'Far more easily than I believe Naomi on the subject.' He threw a smile over his shoulder as Megan drew him from the room. 'Until tomorrow then, Scheherazade. I missed my story tonight.'

'I'll make it up to you tomorrow,' she promised, then rather wished she hadn't when Bran's deepening smile won him a strange look from Megan as she hustled him from the room.

CHAPTER SEVEN

Naomi had a very bad night after her visitors left. A combination of restlessness after Bran's lovemaking and guilt over Diana's article scotched all hope of a good night's rest.

'And how are you this morning?' said Megan, when Naomi arrived in the kitchen. 'Should you be up? I was sure you were coming down with a fever last night.'

'I feel a lot better than yesterday,' Naomi assured her, glad Megan had no idea of the exact nature of the 'fever'.

'Now you eat a good breakfast, my girl, and don't overdo it today. Bran won't mind if the book doesn't get finished dead on the dot, I'm sure.'

Naomi smiled wryly. 'But *I* will. I've got my proper job to get back to, remember.'

Despite her usual post-migraine fragility, Naomi worked with a will once she was back at the word processor. The time passed so quickly that she looked up in surprise when Megan came to say Bran had given orders for Naomi to join him for coffee.

'Is it that late already?' she said blankly.

'I told you not to overdo it,' scolded Megan. 'Off you go and have a break.'

'About time,' complained Bran when she arrived in the studio. 'Megan wouldn't let me interrupt you before.'

'I wanted to make up for lost time yesterday.' Naomi

113

crossed the room to touch his hand in her usual greeting. 'How are you this morning?'

'All the better for being with you.' He retained her hand, pulling her over to the sofa. 'Come and sit down and tell me how you feel today, and how you look, and what you're wearing and anything else you think will be of the slightest interest to me.'

Naomi chuckled. 'I feel fine and I look pretty much the same as usual in jeans, navy jersey and pink shirt. There. May I pour the coffee now, please? Now I've stopped I realise how much I've been looking forward to it.'

'To what?' he said instantly. 'The coffee, or being with me?'

'Both,' she said reluctantly, then caught her breath at the look of triumph on Bran's face.

'You've admitted it,' he crowed, then released her hand. 'All right, pour the blasted coffee if you must. Tell me how you felt last night.'

Naomi filled his cup with an unsteady hand. 'When, in particular?'

'When Megan interrupted us, woman! Lord knows I'm fond of her, but I could have wished her anywhere else at that particular juncture.'

Naomi stirred sugar into the coffee and handed him the mug. 'Perhaps it's just as well she arrived when she did.'

'Why? Were you afraid I'd overcome your objections and have my wicked way with you?' He turned in her direction, his eyes glittering a challenge which brought a hectic flush to her face.

'The thing that really frightened me was my lack of any objection at all,' Naomi told him with painful honesty.

Bran sat very still, the laughter fading from his face. 'Does that mean you'd have let me stay last night?'

She breathed in deeply. 'I don't know. I hope I'd have found the strength from somewhere to call a halt. So from now until I leave I've decided the best plan is to avoid situations like last night.'

'You mean you won't let me into your bedroom.'

'The question won't arise. I don't get migraines very often.'

'What makes you think I need an excuse?'

'Not what. Who.'

Bran gave her a twisted smile. 'Ah, I see. You think I wouldn't dare under Megan's eagle eye.'

'Exactly.' Naomi shivered audibly. 'If such an unlikely situation should arise — which it won't — she'd forgive you, but she'd never forgive me.'

'Why should she forgive *me*?'

'Because,' said Naomi very quietly, 'I'm sure that Megan, like all the other women you know, would forgive you anything.'

Bran reached out a peremptory hand. 'Does that go for you too?' he asked huskily.

Naomi put her hand in his. 'I don't know. And since I'm unlikely to be put to the test I never will.'

Bran's fingers tightened on hers. 'Something tells me I'd forgive *you*, Naomi, whatever your trespass.'

Blood flew to Naomi's face. Guilt and longing took her breath away as his hand tightened, pulling her towards him and into his arms. He rubbed his cheek against hers, eyes tightly closed as he registered the smooth heat of it against his own. He drew a deep, ragged breath as he felt her yield, then his seeking mouth slid along the line of her jaw to find her mouth and she trembled against him as their lips met and locked and parted only when neither could exist any longer without oxygen.

Naomi buried her head against his shoulder, her

entire body vibrating with their combined heartbeat as she fought with the urge to confess.

Bran smoothed a hand over her hair, breathing rapidly. 'I meant it, Naomi.'

She stiffened, and drew away to look up into his face. 'Meant what?'

'That I'd forgive you anything.'

From somewhere she managed to find the strength to stand up. 'I doubt that, somehow,' she said in a stifled voice. 'You're only human, Bran.'

'Isn't that the truth,' he said grimly.

'And I'm human, too, Bran.' She touched his shoulder fleetingly to take the sting from her words. 'So let's avoid passages like last night — and this morning — from now on.'

His face set. 'That's what you want?'

'No, it isn't,' she said honestly. 'But it's what I'm asking, just the same.'

Bran raised a sardonic eyebrow. 'I don't make promises I can't keep, Naomi.' He shrugged irritably. 'And now I suppose you're going to run away again, back to that bloody machine. You'd think it was human — and male — the way I'm getting to resent the damn thing.'

Naomi chuckled breathlessly. 'I'll see you at dinner.'

'I thought I'd stay in today and see you at lunch as well,' he said swiftly, his smile so persuasive she badly wanted to say yes.

'No way. I'm not stopping for lunch.'

'Cruel woman.'

'No, just sensible,' she said firmly, hoping Bran had no idea what a fight she had to be sensible where he was concerned.

Naomi won the battle for the next two days, while she finished off the draft of *The Flight of the Crow*. She dined with Bran as usual, read the day's work back to him afterwards, before going on to read excerpts from whatever book he wanted, though often all Bran really wanted to do was just talk, or listen to music, but always with his hand holding hers, as though the contact was necessary to his morale.

'You're my night-light in the dark, Naomi,' he told her.

'I'm glad I'm useful,' she countered, secretly touched to the heart.

'I'd like you to be more than that,' he sighed moodily, 'but you frighten me.'

'*Frighten* you? How can I possibly do that?'

'I'm afraid that if I demand more than just this small, comforting hand in mine you'll run away. And don't rabbit on about being sensible,' he added testily, 'or I won't be responsible for my actions.'

'Then I won't,' she said calmly. 'How about some music?'

'All right, as long as it's something lively and unromantic. A man can only stand so much, *cariad*!'

Time was flying by far too swiftly for Naomi. Soon, much too soon, it would be time to leave. The draft was almost finished, and, although Bran had asked her to stay to the weekend as originally planned, she knew her best course was to leave Gwal-y-Ddraig the moment there was no excuse to linger. Bran, with unconcealed reluctance, had refrained from actually making love to her as she asked, but there were more ways of making love, she discovered, than mere physical contact. Bran had a love for poetry that held an allure for her mind almost as powerful as the irresistible hint of dependency beneath his virility.

Naomi had gone to bed earlier than usual the following evening, worn out by the strain of hours alone with Bran in the studio. That he wanted to make love to her was an unspoken, living undercurrent between them the entire time they were together. Naomi knew that she had only to relax her guard for a moment and she would be in Bran's arms and that would be that. If he really set out to make love to her she had no illusion about her own opposition, either to him or to herself, which was more to the point. She could fight one of them, but not both.

Naomi was tossing and turning restlessly in bed, cursing herself for leaving Bran so early, when a knock on the door made her heart thump in her chest.

'Come in,' she called, her throat suddenly dry. Then she saw Megan's head pop round the door and disappointment swamped her in a cold, humiliating tide.

'Thank goodness you're still awake, love,' said Megan, looking so distraught that Naomi shot upright in bed, her eyes anxious.

'Something wrong, Megan?'

The other woman nodded, wiping tears from a face creased with worry. 'It's Haydn.'

Not Bran. Naomi fought to hide her relief. 'Tal's brother? What's the matter?'

'He's been in a car accident — some joyrider out in a stolen car went into him near Newport earlier this evening. They've taken him into the Gwent — the hospital there. Tal's his next of kin now, you see, which is why the hospital just rang him.' Tears ran suddenly down Megan's cheeks. 'They said Haydn's poorly. And you know what that means, in hospital terms.'

Naomi jumped out of bed and put her arm round Megan. 'I'm so sorry. Is there anything I can do? Anything at all?'

Megan sniffed hard. 'Well, there is, but it seems such a cheek to ask. I've just been to see Bran and he says it's all right if we both go, Tal and me, I mean. But I don't like leaving Bran on his own ——'

'But he's not on his own,' said Naomi, pulse racing. 'I'm here. In any case Bran will be all right overnight. And I'll see to his breakfast if that's all that's worrying you.'

'There's good you are!'

Not good at all, thought Naomi, her cheeks hot. 'Nonsense. You can't let Tal go on his own. But please ring at some stage and let me know how things are.'

Megan, all at sea for once with worry, assured Naomi she'd keep her posted, then hurried off downstairs. Naomi jumped out of bed and pulled on her dressing-gown to follow her, to see if there was anything she could do to speed the grief-stricken pair on their way. She met Tal in the hall, obviously on his way back from the studio. He looked drawn and worried as he assured her that Bran needed nothing until next morning.

'It's funny, see, love,' he said, hurrying with her into the kitchen. 'I'm the one who's always under the weather, with this chest of mine. Haydn's usually fit as a fiddle. Salt of the earth, my brother — he didn't deserve this!'

There was no sign of Bran as Naomi helped Megan and Tal collect their things. She waved them off down the drive, then went back into the house and locked the door, casting a yearning look towards the corridor that led to the studio. But, she reminded herself stringently, she had been the one with all the high-minded objections. They might have the house unexpectedly to themselves, but it couldn't be allowed to make any difference.

Naomi went upstairs slowly, her eyes on the oblong of light coming from the corridor. But no tall, familiar figure materialised there to halt her progress. With a sigh she went back to her bedroom and closed the door, then got into bed. But before she could switch off the light the door opened and Bran stood there in silence, his hand against the lintel to orientate himself. He took two steps into the room, then closed the door behind him and walked slowly towards the bed. Naomi leapt out of bed to meet him halfway across the room, sliding her arms round his waist and laying her cheek against the gratifying thunder of his heartbeat as his arms locked her against him.

'I almost didn't come,' he said, his voice harsh with emotion as he leaned his cheek against the crown of her head.

'I almost came to you,' she told him, and felt him relax, shaking with sudden laughter against her.

'Such honesty, *cariad*!' He bent his head and she raised hers eagerly, meeting his mouth with her own. Her hands went up to encircle his neck and Bran stopped and lifted her in his arms. 'I couldn't carry you up that stair in the studio, Naomi, but I can manage it from here to your bed.' And, as sure-footed as though he could see, he walked to the bed and laid her down on it, then straightened and stood still.

She stared up at him uncertainly, and, sensitive as always to her mood, he smiled exultantly as he stripped off his dressing-gown before sliding into bed beside her to take her into his arms.

'Surely you didn't think I was about to turn tail and go back again,' he said mockingly.

'I did wonder for a moment,' she admitted in a stifled voice.

Bran pulled her closer, his lips warm against her cheek. 'Naomi, I know you have reservations about all this, but when Megan and Tal were sent for tonight, grief though it might mean for them, I took it as fate. That this was meant to be for you and me. As must be blindingly obvious right this minute, I want you, Naomi, so badly I'm going out of my mind.'

'It would be a pity for that to happen,' she said sedately. 'After all, it's such an *informed* mind.'

Bran laughed and rolled over to capture her beneath him. 'Ah, Naomi, what a delight you are!'

Having just been told that Bran was on fire with the urge to make love to her, Naomi tensed, expecting an onslaught designed to bring him relief as quickly as humanly possible. But Bran was no callow youth, at the mercy of his own senses. When he kissed her there was tenderness as well as urgency in the caress, so that she yielded to the desire flowering inside her, responding ardently to the persuasive caresses of his hands as they moved in a slow, relishing journey over her body.

'Ah, *cariad*,' he breathed against her lips. 'If you only knew how much I've yearned to do this, and this ——' He moved his head lower, his lips searching for the pulse that throbbed at the base of her throat. When his descending mouth encountered the slight obstruction of her nightgown he made no move to push it aside, but returned his attention to her mouth, his lips and probing, subtle tongue winning him such rewards that Bran tensed and raised his head a fraction.

'I'm trying my hardest to take time over this, my lovely,' he said hoarsely. 'Having gone so long without such glorious solace, I'm determined to prolong the experience to the full.'

Naomi ran her fingertips over his shoulders and down his spine, at the same time embarking on a series of swift, feather-soft kisses along his hard jaw. 'Amen to that,' she agreed piously.

Bran's breath rasped in his chest. 'But there's a problem, *cariad*. Such flattering co-operation, welcome and delightful though it is, makes delay rather difficult.'

Naomi threw her hands wide instantly. 'Then I'll be good.'

'Not too good,' he whispered, and kissed her smiling mouth, at the same time running his hand down her ribs over the thin lawn which covered them, his fingertips lingering as they outlined her hips before moving down to slim bare thighs which tensed at his touch.

'Have you ever heard of Dafydd ap Gwilym?' he asked, surprising her.

Naomi gave a stifled laugh. 'No. Is he a delaying tactic?'

'By no means.' He clicked his tongue in disapproval. 'He's only the greatest poet of medieval Wales, I'd have you know.'

'Oh, *that* Dafydd ap Gwilym,' she said pertly, wriggling closer.

'Irreverent Saxon! Besides, medieval he might be, but his poetry's extraordinarily apt at this moment in time.' Bran's arms tightened round her, his deep voice seductively ragged, its lilt more pronounced than usual as he began to woo her with words composed centuries before, yet so tailored to the moment that he could have written them himself that very day.

'"Grant me, dear life, this lover's blessing",' began Bran slowly, in a tone which sent shivers down her spine, '"a conquering kiss, a swift undressing".' He dispensed with the nightgown deftly and moved his hands slowly over her body, as if memorising every curve of it.

'"A wild delight, a long caressing",' he went on hoarsely, '"and all to end in heart's possessing".'

Bran lay half beside and half over her naked, expectant body, his eyes tightly closed as his hands continued on their caressing journey. With a sinuous movement he slid lower in the bed, his lips roving over her lifting breasts, drawing a choked cry from her as his mouth closed over first one hard, erect tip and then the other. Her heart hammered as his exploring hands found the secret place which opened to his caresses with such abandon that he replaced his probing, insistent fingers with his lips and tongue and brought Naomi to sudden, throbbing fulfilment, taking her so much by storm that she gasped and cried out and arched her body in its throes.

Bran laughed exultantly and caught her close in his arms, kissing her with all the triumph of a conqueror who had stormed the citadel. Naomi clutched at him wildly.

'But it was *you* who wanted ——'

'And intend to have,' he promised, and began his assault on her senses all over again, but this time she retaliated, instigating a counter-attack of her own with hands which stroked and teased, coming close to, but never quite touching, the part of him he wanted her to touch most.

'Little devil,' he panted, kissing her, then groaned as she wriggled close and captured him at last in a caress which brought a groan of such anguish from him that she thought he was hurt and threw her arms round him, at which point Bran Llewellyn could no longer face delay and entered, finally, the portal that opened to him with unrestrained welcome. Their bodies met and matched each other in quickly found harmony, all Bran's efforts to delay abandoned in triumph as he accepted Naomi's surrender as his right, taking her with him to heights of pleasure never imagined in her wildest dreams.

Afterwards the long, tranquil aftermath of their loving, held close in Bran's arms, was as beautiful and

wonderful in its own way to Naomi as the heat and
frenzy of the loving itself. She tightened her arm round
his waist and Bran sighed with pleasure.

'If this were fiction,' he said, moving his lips over
her face, 'the shock of such a superlative experience
would have brought my sight back.'

Naomi hoisted herself up on an elbow to smooth
back the black hair from his damp forehead. 'Oh, I
see. That's why you were so hot to make love to me.
You hoped I'd provide a miracle cure!'

He pulled her down to him again, threading one
hand into her hair to draw her face against his throat.
'You know damn well it wasn't, witch! I made love to
you because I was about to expire if I didn't. And
don't tell me I'd have felt differently if I could see you
because I flatly refuse to believe it.'

Naomi lay quietly against him, making no effort to
contradict him for once, then she reached up and
turned out the light. 'There. Now I can't see you
either.' She moved her hand down his chest delicately.
'I'll let my fingers act for my eyes.'

'If you do,' said Bran in a constrained voice, 'I won't
answer for the consequences.'

'Shall I stop, then?'

'No — *duw*, no!'

Naomi laughed with sudden, confident elation, and
went on with her exploration, until suddenly he thrust
her on her back and ran his hands down her spine to
cup her and lift her and make love to her again. This
time their quest was shorter and even more tumul-
tuous, so glorious and overwhelming that afterwards
when they lay quiet in each other's arms exhaustion
overtook Naomi and she fell deeply asleep.

CHAPTER EIGHT

WAKING in Bran's arms at dawn was a new and dangerously blissful experience. Naomi lay very still, aware in every nerve of Bran's warmth, of the brush of his thick black hair on her shoulder, the weight of the imprisoning leg he'd thrown across hers in the night. She moved slightly, and he murmured, his arms tightening a fraction, and she lay motionless, abandoning all idea of getting up. Just this once she would allow herself the luxury of lying here with him, cut off from the rest of the world in an oasis of miraculous privacy.

Naomi lay looking at the light as it brightened the room, and relived the events of the night, suddenly mindful that her bliss was the direct result of Haydn Griffiths's accident. Remorsefully she wondered how he was faring, and when Megan would ring to let them know.

When the telephone rang at a few minutes past seven Naomi, even though expecting it, jumped out of her skin, disturbing Bran, who tightened his arms involuntarily. When Naomi placed a restraining finger on his lips he slackened his hold just enough to let her take the receiver from its cradle, then threatened her composure badly by planting a series of kisses on her bare back as she gave the Gwal-y-Ddraig number.

Megan sounded strained and tired as she reported that Haydn had been operated on in the night and was still unconscious, but by courtesy of a strong constitution had survived his ordeal better than expected.

'I hate to ask this, love,' she said anxiously, 'but could you cope if I stayed down here with Tal today?

He wants to be there when Haydn comes round, you see. It's a terrible cheek, I know, but if you could put up some food for Bran——'

'Megan, *please*. Of course I can, and you mustn't worry about anything here,' said Naomi firmly. 'I'll tell Bran you're staying there until you feel you can leave. Stay as long as you want, and don't worry. I'll take good care of Bran.'

Megan's gratitude was tearful and heartfelt. She sent her love to Bran, issued a stream of instructions, then rang off to hurry back to Tal.

Naomi put the phone down and tried to slide out of bed, but Bran pulled her back under the covers and kept her there by the simple expedient of lying on top of her.

'Stay where you are. How's Haydn?' he asked, and listened intently while Naomi gave him the details.

'Megan will ring later in the day,' she finished breathlessly.

Bran nuzzled his lips against her neck. 'Good—I'm glad Haydn came through all right. Now we can enjoy the day with a clear conscience.'

Naomi tried to wriggle free. 'You can,' she said tartly, 'but I've got work to do.'

'No, you haven't,' he contradicted, holding her still. 'Now we've got the bonus of an extra day to ourselves I'm damned if I'm going to let you waste it at that blasted machine.'

'But——'

'But nothing.' Bran kissed her protesting mouth into silence. 'Naomi,' he said at last, in a tone which sent shivers down her spine, 'did you mean what you said?'

'What did I say?' she whispered.

'You told Megan you'd take care of me.'

'Of course I meant it!' Naomi tried to push him away. 'Look, Bran, if you won't let me go I can't get your breakfast, which is what Megan means by taking care of you.'

'To hell with breakfast. Anyone can make a meal for me. But only you, *cariad*, can provide nourishment for my soul.'

Certain Bran was teasing, that she should laugh and treat his words as a joke, Naomi found herself blinking hard on sudden tears. Bran frowned, his hands sliding into her tangled hair as his lips found the tell-tale dampness on her cheeks, then he found her mouth and kissed her with such demand that all thought of food vanished from Naomi's mind as her body caught fire from his.

Making love in the morning, in the sunlight, when Naomi knew she should have been doing any one of several other things, was an experience which possessed its own individual form of magic. The illicit aura to it all added a new dimension to the experience as Naomi's body answered the thrusting urgency of his, her open, dazzled eyes on Bran's face, watching it mirror the sensations overwhelming him as his body convulsed in the throes of the climax he reached only seconds before her own blotted out everything other than the cataclysm of feeling which engulfed her.

'Stay with me,' he said hoarsely, holding her with arms that bruised, and Naomi kissed him, and clutched him closer, as reluctant as he to break apart.

'With you,' said Bran, a long time later, 'I feel whole. As though I'd found the vital part missing from my life.'

A shiver ran through Naomi and Bran held her closer.

'What is it?'

'Someone walked over my grave.' She detached herself with determination. 'And now I *must* get up,

Bran Llewellyn. I need a bath and breakfast and about a gallon of tea.'

'What an unromantic creature you are, to be sure,' he mocked, and got to his feet, stretching, totally unselfconscious of his splendid nudity.

'Someone has to be practical,' she muttered, cheeks hot as she thrust his towelling robe into his hand before scrambling into her own. 'If you'll give me a few minutes in the bath while you get back to the studio I'll cook breakfast afterwards and bring it in to you.'

'I'd much rather share your bath,' said Bran, fumbling with his belt. 'And don't look at me like that!'

'Like what?'

'I don't need sight to know there's disapproval in those long, dark eyes of yours.'

'How do you know my eyes are long?'

'By touch, of course. Just as I know your nose tilts a little and your mouth is wide, with lips so full and sweet I can't resist them.' He smiled, turning her bones to water. 'I know the size and delectable shape of your breasts, and the curve of your hips and the sleek, satin feel of your thighs——'

'Stop it!' said Naomi, her face burning. 'Go away, do. I'll be with you as soon as I can.'

'Hurry up, then!' He felt for the doorknob. 'Until Megan and Tal get back, time apart is time wasted.' He held out his hand. 'Come here.'

Naomi went to him and took the hand, only to be pulled into Bran's arms and kissed at length before she was finally released.

'Fifteen minutes,' he ordered.

'You'll be lucky!'

Naomi rushed through a shower and dressed at top speed, sprayed herself with perfume and tied up her damp hair with a ribbon, then flew downstairs.

In the kitchen she worked rapidly, making coffee for Bran and tea for herself, grilling bacon, slicing bread and breaking eggs into a bowl. Before she could start cooking them Bran came into the room and closed the door, standing against it.

'I'm nearly ready,' said Naomi, surprised. 'If you'll go along to the studio I'll bring your breakfast in a minute.'

'No, you won't! I refuse to let you carry trays when I can perfectly well eat in here. Megan won't allow it, but you will, *cariad*, won't you?'

'I suppose so. It would be easier, I'll admit. Come and sit at the table.'

Bran remained just inside the door, smiling wryly. 'I require a navigator. Megan hasn't let me in here since the accident—afraid I'll do myself lasting injury with her egg-whisk, or something.'

Naomi flew to him to take his hand. 'Allow me,' she said jauntily, and led him to the chair at the head of the table. 'There you are—chairman of the board. Now talk to me while I work.'

Bran lounged back, legs outstretched, his hands relaxed on the arms of the old Windsor carver. He looked rested and vital in denims and bulky green sweatshirt, his eyes following her movements as though he could see as well as hear her, as she quickly laid the table.

'First of all,' he said huskily, 'let's talk about last night.'

Naomi frowned, suddenly still. 'Last night?'

'Yes. The most wonderful, glorious, fulfilling night of my entire life,' said Bran with emphasis. 'I want you to know just how much it meant to me to have you welcome me into your arms like that.'

Naomi began to whip the eggs savagely. 'In contrast to Allegra's rejection, you mean.'

'Hell, no!' Bran looked thunderstruck. 'I never gave a thought to Allegra—nor any other woman. Last night there was just you and me and the incredible experience we shared. Or am I taking too much for granted?' His face suddenly darkened. 'Maybe it wasn't the same for you.'

'Of course it was,' said Naomi breathlessly. 'And you know it.' Her entire body hot at the mere recollection, she doggedly chopped hot bacon into the scrambled eggs and transferred them to hot plates. She put them down on the table, poured orange juice into their glasses, then sat down beside the man who sat with closed eyes, the lines evident again in his brooding face.

'How do I know you're telling the truth?' he demanded.

For answer Naomi leaned across and kissed him at length on the mouth. 'Does that convince you?' she enquired, straightening, but Bran reached up an unerring hand and brought her face down to his so that he could return the kiss with interest.

'Somewhat,' he said, releasing her. 'Indulge me in a little more convincing after breakfast.'

'Would you kindly start eating?' she said tartly, settling back into her place. 'I haven't gone to all this trouble just to watch the eggs grow cold.'

Bran grinned and did as she said, refusing Naomi's offer to turn on the radio. 'No—talk to me instead. After breakfast you can read bits from the papers if you would.'

'Certainly. Anything to oblige,' said Naomi demurely, surprised and secretly rather embarrassed to find she was ravenous once she'd begun on her own meal.

It was well into the morning before Bran agreed to

return to the studio, on condition that Naomi joined him there as soon as possible.

'I'll be an hour,' she said firmly.

'An hour! What the hell are you going to do?' he demanded wrathfully.

'Some tidying up. I couldn't face Megan if she came home to a messy house.'

Bran sighed, exasperated. 'If you must, you must — but get a move on. I need you a damn sight more than the house does.'

Deeply gratified, Naomi whisked through a few basic chores, then ran to her room to tidy herself. Her eyes gleamed as they studied her reflection. A life of illicit pleasure was definitely good for her looks, she thought satirically, not daring to imagine how she'd look once she'd returned to her old life. A life without Bran Llewellyn.

'At last!' growled Bran, when she joined him in the studio. 'What the devil have you been doing? Spring-cleaning the entire house?'

'Actually,' said Naomi severely, 'I'm ten minutes earlier than promised. What do I have to do to win your approval, may I ask?'

Bran held up his arms. 'You know very well. Come here.'

'Certainly not. I'm going to read to you from today's paper,' she said firmly, and sat down on the sofa beside him.

He flung away into the corner of the sofa and leaned his head back. 'Oh, very well.'

Peace reigned for several minutes while Naomi chose items she hoped would interest Bran. When it became obvious that he was waiting instead of listening she gave up.

'All right, you win. Shall I switch on the radio, or would you prefer one of your CDs?'

'Neither. I want you to sit on my knee.'

'Possibly,' she said, secretly elated by his open need of her.

'But you won't. All right, spoilsport, let's go for a walk, then,' he said, surprising her. 'There's a green, lush smell of spring coming through the windows, and I want out of here for a while. Come and be my guide. We can take the mobile phone in case Megan rings.'

Naomi was only too happy to stroll hand in hand with Bran in the gardens, quick to anticipate any pitfall for him, counting steps when they went down from the terrace past the bluebell wood to the lawn which Bran told her had once been a bowling green. They sat close together on one of the stone benches, beneath the green, spreading shelter of a giant beech tree, while Bran tried to identify all the different scents assailing his newly sensitive nostrils.

'I never realised before how many different components make up one particular smell,' he observed, 'or truly appreciated the pleasure of warm sun on my skin.'

'Mmm,' agreed Naomi contentedly, 'it's heavenly out here in the sun this morning. I've got my eyes closed, too, to keep you company.'

Bran's arm tightened round her waist. 'You know I could almost cope with the way things are on a permanent basis with you to make up the deficit, Naomi. Now don't go all shy and stiff on me, I don't intend remaining blind, believe me. But having you here with me this last couple of weeks has made a hell of a difference.'

'Probably you'd have felt the same whoever came to work for you,' said Naomi with constraint.

Bran said something brief, rude and explicit in contradiction. 'Last night, when I mentioned my soul,' he went on very quietly, 'I wasn't talking complete nonsense, Naomi. My father had quite a good voice, and one of my earliest recollections is hearing him sing a song about a blind man. I've been thinking about it a lot since you arrived on the scene, especially the last line, which said something about God taking away his eyes so his soul might see.'

Naomi gazed up into his open, glittering eyes, then turned away sharply, suppressing the urge to blurt out the confession which would wreck their newfound harmony.

'What I do see,' went on Bran, holding her closer, 'is that before the accident I was too materialistic. I wanted possessions like this house, and a flash car, and a high-profile lifestyle, so I accepted commissions to paint boring people because it earned me money. I took the easy way out.'

'But the portraits won recognition which lets you do what you want now, surely? Besides,' added Naomi, 'it was a commission that brought you Allegra, I seem to remember.'

'A good argument for never painting a portrait again!' Familiar, cynical lines replaced the visionary look on Bran's face, and impulsively Naomi reached up to kiss them away.

'Let's go back to the house,' he whispered, his hands sliding up beneath her sweater.

Naomi pushed him away firmly. 'No. Let's stay here in the fresh air a little longer, then I'll make you some lunch.'

There was an idyllic quality to their time together as the day wore on. Naomi made sandwiches in the kitchen, while Bran lounged at the head of the table. They talked incessantly, about Naomi's job and her friends, about some of the people Bran had painted, others he'd known in the village of his birth. Then after lunch Megan rang again. Tal's brother was recovering, but weak and full of tubes, she reported, then asked anxiously if Naomi could manage until after visiting time that evening.

Naomi told her emphatically that it was no problem at all, sent her good wishes to Tal, then handed the phone over to Bran, who added his assurances, teasing Megan to allay her anxiety, and telling her to stay at the hospital with Tal as long as she liked.

'Put up at a hotel and come back tomorrow, if you like,' he said casually, grinning in Naomi's direction at her sharp intake of breath. He listened intently for a moment or two, then smiled again, in triumph this time. 'Of course you can, Megan, *bach*. Everthing's fine here, Naomi's doing a yeoman job, and don't worry, I'll pay her some overtime. Take it easy now, buy Haydn some grapes from me, and we'll see you at lunchtime tomorrow.'

Naomi stood very still as Bran put down the phone. 'Megan's not coming back today?'

Bran leaned back in his chair, his eyes gleaming through his lowered lashes. 'No. Tal's got some cousins in Newport. They went to visit Haydn and suggested Megan and Tal stay with them overnight so they can call in at the hospital before coming back here tomorrow.'

Naomi sat down at the table abruptly. 'Bran, there's something I must tell you——'

'No need,' he interrupted, suddenly serious. 'All I ask is your company, Naomi. I'd be lying if I said I didn't want to make love to you, too. What man wouldn't? But just having you with me to talk to, to be near me, is enough if you want it that way.'

'Not to mention a shot at cooking your dinner,' said Naomi with difficulty.

'Not if it means hours spent in preparation! Open a tin of something—soup, beans, anything.' Bran stretched out a hand, and Naomi put hers into it. 'Come back to the studio and listen to some music, then we'll go out for a stroll in the garden again.'

Naomi, who'd been on the very brink of telling Bran all about Diana and her article, cast confession to the winds. It would be madness to spoil the unexpected gift of an extra day alone with Bran. There would be time enough for sackcloth and ashes. Afterwards.

The dreamlike quality of the day persisted. Afterwards Naomi could never remember what music they listened to, or what books and films they discussed. There was only her pleasure in Bran's company, and his, openly displayed, in hers. Throughout the long warm afternoon Bran made no move to touch her other than to hold her hand. But always there was an underlying *frisson* of excitement, the memory of their night vivid and unforgettable beneath the badinage and laughter.

Dinner was a lamb and leek pie from Megan's freezer, accompanied by tiny potatoes in their jackets. They ate it informally at the kitchen table, with seedless grapes and a wedge of Caerphilly cheese to round it off.

'I'm not much of a cook, I'm afraid,' confessed Naomi, as she helped Bran to cheese. 'I was relieved when Megan told me to raid the freezer. She's got enough in there for an army.'

'She's manic about emergencies,' said Bran. 'I keep telling her this place is off-limits to visitors, but she keeps the place stocked with food just the same, convinced people will find it and drop in.'

'She'd be shocked to see us here like this at the kitchen table,' said Naomi, getting up to clear away. 'She probably expected me to serve the meal in state in the dining-room.'

Bran laughed, and leaned back in the chair, stretching luxuriously. 'What Megan doesn't know can't hurt her.'

'Isn't that the truth!'

Suddenly the atmosphere was different.

'You mean she wouldn't approve of the way we spent last night — and this morning?' asked Bran bluntly.

'Since I don't intend to ask, I'll never know.' Naomi began loading the dishwasher rather noisily.

Bran said nothing more for a while, until there was a lull in the activity. 'Have you finished?' he asked.

'Yes. I'll just make some coffee——'

'To hell with the coffee. Let's just go back to the studio and listen to some soothing music, and talk for a while. I've got something to ask.'

Naomi put her hand into the one Bran held out towards her as he got up from the table, her eyes troubled as they searched his face, which was as informative as a wooden mask as they went along the corridor to the studio. They found the big room filled with an eerie green twilight. Gathering clouds had replaced the sunshine of the afternoon, imparting an air of menace which sent Naomi hurrying to switch on lamps, shivering as she described it to Bran.

'Are you cold?' he asked.

'Not really.'

'Same person tramping on your grave again?'

'Something like that.'

'Come here, then.' Bran reached out a seeking arm and hooked her close. 'What's wrong, Naomi?'

'You said that you had something to ask.'

'Is that all? It's just that I realise you'll be finished on the book tomorrow. I want you to stay on for a while afterwards instead of running away the minute you've handed over the draft.'

'I promised to stay with my parents——' she began, but he interrupted her swiftly.

'Visit them the following weekend. You can drive back to London early Monday morning.'

'I can't do that,' she said reluctantly. 'If I stay — if I stay until then I'll have to leave on Sunday evening at the latest.'

'Better than nothing,' he said grudgingly, and caught her chin in his hand, turning her face up to his seeking mouth. 'Now,' he said against her lips, 'no more talking, just kiss me!'

Naomi obeyed without question, locking her hands behind his neck as his mouth met hers, suddenly as desperate as Bran for the touch of his mouth and his hands and the feel of his body against her as he swung her up on to his lap and held her hard against his chest.

His breathing quickened as he moved his mouth over face and down her throat, his fingers skilful as he flicked open her shirt and searched for the small clasp between her shoulder blades. As her breasts filled his hands he gave a groan and buried his face against her, his tongue flicking her nipples into erect, quivering response and Naomi gasped and clutched his head closer.

Suddenly Bran set her on her feet and stood up, his hand holding hers in an iron grip as he drew her towards the stair leading to his bedroom.

Naomi hesitated, pulling back for a moment, but he jerked her into his arms and kissed her again, then laughed against her open, protesting mouth.

'I'll carry you up if you prefer——'

'Bran, no——'

'I agree, better on your own two feet, my lovely.'

'That's not what I meant,' she said desperately. 'I don't know that I want this.'

Bran stood stock-still, all the heat and anticipation draining from his face as he released her. 'You're lying, Naomi. I may not be able to see, but I could feel your response.'

'It's nothing to do with that.' She tidied herself with shaking hands, willing him to understand. 'Last night was an accident, unpremeditated, something we hadn't planned or expected to happen. Tonight it's—well, it's different.'

Bran thrust a hand through his hair, looking distraught. 'Naomi, what possible harm can it do to anyone if we share a bed tonight? Or any other night, if it comes to that?'

'It's not something I do,' she muttered doggedly.

'You think I don't know that?' He turned away, feeling his way to the sofa. He slumped down, his face set in the familiar bitter lines. 'I thought we'd found something very special together. Or were you just taking pity on a blind man last night?' he added, in a voice that slashed at her like a razor.

'No, Bran, no!' she said in horror, and flew to him, sitting on his lap and wreathing her arms round his neck all in one movement. She kissed him in an agony of reassurance, oblivious of the pain when his arms closed round her like a vice.

'Then come with me. Now.' Bran got to his feet, still holding her in his arms. He set her on her feet and hauled her with him across the room, pushing her up the stair ahead of him. Beside his bed Bran halted, his breath hot on her face as he bent to take her in his arms. 'Surely you can tell this isn't just sex, *cariad*?' he demanded, in a voice so harsh with emotion that she threw her arms round his waist and hugged him close, nodding violently, unable to trust her voice.

Bran rubbed his cheek against hers. 'I need you, Naomi. Before you came I was wallowing in despair, sorry for myself, Now I know I can cope with life whether my sight comes back or not.'

CHAPTER NINE

NAOMI, glad that Bran couldn't see her heavy eyes, insisted on starting work next morning immediately breakfast was over, determined to restore some kind of normality to life before Megan got back.

'That won't be for hours yet. Let's just go back to bed,' Bran suggested as she steered him through the kitchen door.

Naomi paused, eyeing his rested, confident face narrowly. 'Why? Is it an urge to make up for lost time — because you've been sex-starved for longer than usual?'

Bran scowled. 'No, it bloody well isn't. I thought I made that clear last night. And,' he added softly, 'you may like to know that just having you in my arms, curled up against me in the night, was almost as much pleasure as having you writhing beneath me like a wild thing as I made love to you.'

Naomi breathed in sharply, her colour high. 'If you're going to say things like that, I'm off to the study.'

Bran turned, holding out his arms. 'Can't I persuade you to stay?'

'All too easily.'

'Tell me how and I will.'

'You know exactly how,' she said tartly. 'Anyway, Megan said she'll be home by twelve. I want to get an hour in before she does. I've liberated one of her cartons of soup from the freezer, and made some sandwiches so she won't have to get lunch the minute she comes through the door.'

'A very paragon of virtue!'

'Hardly!' Naomi reached up and give him a swift kiss, then dodged out of the way quickly. 'See you later.'

'Read me something from the papers first,' he said imperiously.

'Afterwards. Listen to the radio instead.'

'I'd much rather listen to you, *cariad*.' His smile flipped her heart over in her chest, but Naomi struck doggedly to her guns.

'I've only got an hour's work to do and I'll be finished! Do whatever you used to do before I came here.'

Bran's face turned bleak suddenly. 'And, presumably, what I shall have to do again. When you go.'

'Well, I'm not going yet,' she said briskly, secretly devastated at the very thought.

Once at her desk, Naomi worked hard, fighting her way through a fog of heavy lassitude after the long, unforgettable night in Bran's bed. The aftermath had left her depressed and anticlimactic, harrowed by the knowledge that tonight, and every other night for the foreseeable future, she would sleep alone.

To keep her brain occupied Naomi worked doggedly through until the last of the tapes was typed, edited and printed, managing to finish just as Megan and Tal returned. She stacked the manuscript neatly together when she heard the car, and ran through the kitchen to the yard at the back to welcome the couple home.

In a flurry of greetings, Megan gave the latest news on Haydn's progress, while Tal went straight off to find Bran.

Megan was full of questions as she parked her bags in the kitchen and took her coat off. She reached for the striped apron hanging behind the door almost in one movement as Naomi assured her Bran had been well taken care of in her absence.

'I know that, love,' said Megan, looking Naomi in the eye. 'Otherwise I wouldn't have stayed in Newport so long.'

Naomi flushed a little as she waved a hand at the refrigerator. 'I made some sandwiches earlier on and left them in there, and I took some of your soup from the freezer and put it in a pan. And there's some pie left from last night. I thought I'd save you having to cook lunch, at least. You must be very tired.'

'That's lovely of you, Naomi—though we had quite a good night's rest last night in Gwyneth's house in Newport.'

'Good. I'm glad Mr Griffiths is on the mend.'

'Aren't we all?' said Megan with a heartfelt sigh. 'How's the book going, then?'

Naomi told her she'd completed it only minutes before. 'One more bit to read back to Bran, then I've finished.'

'He's not going to be easy to live with once you're gone,' said Megan gloomily. 'No sign of his sight coming back, I suppose?'

Naomi shook her head. 'But it will, Megan, I'm sure of that.'

'*Duw*, I hope so!' Megan shook off her momentary depression. 'Right, I'll go and see Bran before doing a tray for you both.' She eyed Naomi closely. 'It's you who look tired, mind. Haven't you been sleeping well?'

'Not very,' said Naomi, with perfect truth, and escaped, pink-cheeked, to join Bran.

She found him sitting bolt upright at one end of the sofa, a still, waiting air about him whicn set her mental alarm bells ringing.

'Naomi,' he stated.

'Sorry I kept you waiting.' She sat beside him, poised to serve the meal. 'Did Megan think you'd survived satisfactorily without her?'

'I believe so. She told me you've finished the draft.'

'Yes. After lunch I'll read the last bit back to you, make any alterations you want, and that's it. The job's done. Sandwich?'

'I'm not hungry. Just coffee. Please.'

Naomi eyed him apprehensively as she handed it to him. 'Would you like me to read the last pages to you now?'

'Don't you want to eat first?' he said curtly.

'I'm not hungry either.'

'In that case by all means make a start. Afterwards perhaps you'd spare the time to read a few items from the paper.'

'Yes, of course.' Naomi eyed him despairingly as she reached for the manuscript. Something was horribly wrong. The lover of the night had vanished, replaced by the morose Bran Llewellyn of her first day or two at Gwal-y-Ddraig.

The reading took very little time to complete. Bran nodded afterwards without enthusiasm, brushing aside her offer to make any alterations he wanted. 'It'll do. Some editor from Diadem will probably chop the thing to bits, anyway. Send it off this afternoon.'

'Very well. Anything special you want me to say in the covering letter?'

'No.' Bran reached down beside him for a newspaper and handed it to her. 'Now read this. Tal tells me there's a very interesting article on page five.'

Naomi took the paper, then almost dropped it. Instead of his usual *Times* Bran had given her a copy of the *Chronicle*.

She cleared her throat. 'This isn't your usual paper.'

'No. But Tal gets it whenever he can. He bought one this morning in Newport.'

Naomi's heart thudded in her chest. She'd never thought to ask about the Griffithses' taste in daily papers. She stared at the *Chronicle* in her hand without hope. Diana had sworn her article wouldn't be published until the following week, but it was obvious from Bran's manner that Nemesis was at hand just the same. Nor was it difficult to find the article. Diana's headline hit her right between the eyes. LAIR OF THE DRAGON stood out in bold type above a photograph of the house shot from a distance with a zoom lens.

'You've found the piece?' said Bran.

'Yes,' whispered Naomi.

'Read, then.'

'"Bran Llewellyn,"' began Naomi, then stopped, forced to clear her throat and start again. '"Bran Llewellyn, one of the best artists to come out of Wales since Augustus John, has for years found refuge in the Welsh Marches, where his picturesque country retreat is a far cry from the terraced house in the Rhondda coal-mining village of his birth."'

'A little florid, but so far reasonably accurate,' commented Bran. 'Read on.'

The rest of the article described the exterior of the house and the spiral stair and great north windows of the studio, where the walls displayed some of the artist's work, including a self-portrait never exhibited to the general public. Diana went on to the wild charm of the terraced gardens, mentioned the loyal Welsh couple who looked after Bran, and commiserated on his climbing accident. His social popularity was glossed over rather cleverly, before the article finished with a brief chronicle of the artist's various exhibitions, and the famous faces he'd recorded for posterity, then gave a plug to the forthcoming autobiography 'The Flight of the Crow' to round things off.

The silence in the room was a tangible thing afterwards as Naomi sat shivering and speechless. There was nothing untrue or libellous in the article, but one look at Bran's face was enough to see he was seething with icy rage.

'So,' he said at last, his voice grating, 'I'm getting guilty vibrations, loud and clear, Scheherazade.'

'I — I don't know what you mean.'

'Oh, come on, darling,' he said derisively. 'Let's not play games. When Tal read me the article it didn't take much to identify the source of the reporter's information. If you'd stuck to exteriors and the garden all would have been well. But no one's been inside my studio since it was completed — apart from Megan and Tal, of course. No one else has ever seen the self-portrait, Naomi. And not even the editor at Diadem knows the title I've chosen for the book. The only thing missing is the hottest item of all — my blindness! Why did you spare me that, I wonder?' He clenched his fists, his face a mask of fury. 'Tell me, did *you* take the photograph?'

'No!'

'So someone came trespassing. But it was you who supplied the rest!'

'Yes.'

'I hope they paid you well for it.'

Naomi gasped. 'I didn't do it for money!'

'Why, then?'

'I can't tell you that.'

'You don't need to.' Bran's teeth showed in a tigerish smile. 'I got Tal to put a call through to the *Chronicle* to ask who'd written the article.'

Naomi's shoulders sagged. 'I see.'

'I'm sure you do. Even a blind man like me can

see — now. Miss Diana Barry's lucky to have a sister willing to do a little insider trading.'

Naomi sat with bowed head, unable to say a word.

'Why the hell did you do it?' he demanded.

'Because Diana needed the information,' she said flatly.

'It isn't the article itself that sticks in my throat.' His face set in menacing lines. 'It's the fact that you lied your way in here to get the information. *You*, Naomi — the one person I would have bet my last cent on as honest.'

'Normally I am,' she said bleakly, 'not that I expect you to believe it now. But if I'm in the witness box you may as well know it all. A friend of Diana's arranged for her to do the work for you, but she couldn't take the time off from the *Chronicle*, so she begged me to take her place.'

Bran thrust a hand through his hair convulsively. 'And you agreed?'

'Yes.'

'Willingly?'

'Of course I wasn't willing!'

Bran's mouth tightened. 'Then *why*?'

'Diana believes the article will help her get the promotion she's after,' said Naomi brokenly. 'She — she was a tower of strength to me in the past when I needed help, so I couldn't refuse mine the only time she's ever asked for it. I had three weeks' holiday due so in the end I gave in and agreed to come here and work for you, and at the same time provide her with copy for the article she's convinced is a matter of life and death to her career.'

'So now I know how you come to be here,' Bran said after a protracted, simmering silence. His face was mask-like, the eyes tightly closed. 'And now you've explained I suppose it's just about possible to understand your motives. At least you didn't sell the bloody information for money.' His eyes flew open. 'But what I can't understand,' he said with sudden savagery, 'is why the *hell* you let me make love to you.'

Because I'm madly in love with you and knew I'd regret it forever if I didn't, thought Naomi despairingly. If I'd had any sense I'd have shut the door in your face the other night, blindness or no blindness. It would have made things a lot simpler, one way and another.

'Wasn't it obvious?' she said unsteadily.

'At the time I was fool enough to think so. But I don't any more. Was your idea to soften the blow when I found out? Or was it some strange quixotic idea of paying for the information you'd leaked to your sister?'

'It was neither,' she said, her voice barely above a whisper. 'I know an apology's useless, but I am sorry, Bran. Desperately sorry.'

'So am I,' he said bitterly. 'And not about the publicity—I'm used to that! There's nothing objectionable in the article. Compared with some of the garbage written about me in the past it's bloody flattering.' He flung out a clenched, white-knuckled hand. 'What burns me up is the fact that you were responsible for it. You *used* me, Naomi, infiltrated my house, my confidence, even my bloody bed—and all just to get a story for your sister!'

'No—*please*, it wasn't like that, Bran! What can I do to convince you?'

'Do? I'll tell you exactly what you can do, Miss Judas.' Bran leapt to his feet, putting out a hand to steady himself. 'You can get out of my sight——'

He gave a sudden, wild laugh at the word, and Naomi flinched as though he'd struck her, then backed away before he found out she was crying. Letting the tears run silently down her face, she snatched up the finished manuscript and fled from the studio to sanctuary in the study, where she huddled against the closed door, thrusting her clenched fists against her mouth to stifle her sobs. It was a long time before she was calm enough to mop herself and sit down to type a brief covering letter to Diadem. Afterwards she scribbled her own initials above Bran's name, then sealed the manuscript in a padded envelope and tidied the desk.

Half an hour later she was ready to leave. She took her suitcases down to the hall then went along to the kitchen to seek out Megan, who was in the throes of preparing dinner.

'There's some tea in the pot, love,' said Megan, her eyes on the sauce she was making. 'Bran's gone out for a drive with Tal.'

Naomi cleared her throat. 'I'm leaving now, Megan.'

'*Leaving*?' The other woman spun round, her eyes like saucers. 'Naomi! You look dreadful. Whatever's the matter?'

'The article in the paper,' said Naomi unsteadily. 'It's my fault. My sister wrote it, but—but I gave her the information.'

Megan nodded impatiently. 'I know that. Bran told Tal. But there's no real harm done. There was nothing very terrible in it, for goodness' sake. Bran likes to keep this place private, of course, but anyone could find out he lived here if they tried.'

'But it wasn't *anyone*.' Naomi choked on a sob. 'It was me—and Bran told me to get out of his sight.'

'That's just his temper!' Megan pushed her down in a chair at the table. 'Now just you sit yourself down and drink some nice hot tea.'

Naomi took in a deep, steadying breath. 'Megan, I

just want you to know that I didn't gain by it. Money, I mean.' She blinked hard. 'I just did it for love.'

Megan nodded. 'For your sister.' She handed Naomi a cup. 'Now you drink that, there's a good girl.'

Naomi swallowed the tea, oblivious to its heat, then got to her feet. 'Thank you. I'd better be on my way.'

Megan did her utmost to dissuade her, but Naomi was adamant, desperate to be as far away as possible by the time Bran returned. She gave Megan a quick hug, implored her not to come outside to see her off, then collected her luggage and went out to the car. She gave a last, melancholy look at Gwal-y-Ddraig, then slid behind the wheel and drove as fast as she dared down the steep, winding drive to the road, feeling as if she'd left the vital, living half of her behind.

Naomi returned to London after a few quiet days with her sympathetic but blessedly tactful parents in Cheltenham, to find that Diana had, indeed, been offered the job she was so desperate for; not, ironically enough, because of the article, but because the editor of the *Chronicle* had intended offering her the job all along.

The news came as the last straw. Naomi had spent a long, hot Monday wrestling with the chaos Rupert always managed to create among the accounts while she was away. By the time she saw Diana later that evening she was depressed, irritable and tired, and in no mood to pull her punches when Diana, looking the picture of guilt, told her about the job.

Naomi glared at her sister, incensed. 'Are you telling me that my trip to Wales wasn't even *necessary*?'

Diana nodded, shame-faced. 'Not that the article didn't do me a lot of good—Craig was delighted with it. Plenty of articles have been written about Bran

Llewellyn before, but never about his lair in the Black Mountains. The house gave me a fantastic headline!'

'But why on earth was it published a week earlier than you said? You didn't tell me you were sending a photographer, either,' said Naomi furiously.

Diana gave her a pleading look. 'Sorry. I knew you wouldn't like it, but Phil didn't do any trespassing to get the picture, I promise, and when I showed the article to Craig he wouldn't hear of keeping it back a week. I'm ashamed to say I was too much of a coward to let you know. Besides, you said Bran Llewellyn didn't take the *Chronicle* — I counted on his not seeing it.' She paused, eyeing Naomi's haggard face with concern. 'Good grief, Naomi, you look like death. Was Bran Llewellyn a pig to work for? I *told* you to come away from there, remember.'

'But then you wouldn't have had your precious article,' said Naomi savagely. 'And Bran Llewellyn, just for the record, was fine to work for. Everything was fine until he chanced on the article. He rang the *Chronicle*, found that you wrote the wretched thing, wiped the floor with me and threw me out of his house.'

Diana looked horrified. 'Lord, Naomi — how ghastly for you! Honestly, love, I tried my best to keep the piece back until you were home and dry.'

Naomi made a sharp, dismissive gesture. 'Well, it's done now. I don't want the subject mentioned again. Ever. But next time you want some dirty work done, Miss Hotshot Journalist, you can do it yourself!'

'I'll never ask you to do anything like that again, believe me!' Diana hugged the small, unyielding figure penitently, then stood back, looking down into Naomi's face. 'If you felt that badly about leaking the information why didn't you come back straight away? You could have made some excuse.'

Naomi blushed to the roots of her hair, and pulled away. 'By that time,' she said stiffly, 'I was committed to helping Bran with his manuscript.'

'Bran,' repeated Diana thoughtfully. 'Are you sure you didn't fall head over heels in love with the man?'

'Certainly not,' snapped Naomi.

Diana, obviously unconvinced, had the grace to leave the subject alone. 'I found out about Greg, by the way.'

'Greg.' Naomi looked blank for a moment. 'Oh — right. You needn't have bothered. I don't know why I asked.'

Diana looked deeply relieved. 'I must say it worried me a bit. Why did you want to know?'

'Just curiosity.'

'Good. I'd hate to think you were still hankering after him. Greg, it seems, ditched sexy Susie after only a couple of months in favour of a colleague's bride, then, after making a pig's breakfast of said marriage, flitted off after another Lolita-type even younger than Susie.'

'Busy old Greg,' said Naomi, yawning.

Diana stared at her in wonder. 'It really doesn't matter to you any more, does it?'

'Not a bit. Though I suppose in a way it's some comfort to know it wasn't just me he couldn't stick to.' Naomi yawned again. 'Right. Off you go. And congratulations about the job. I just wish you'd got it sooner. Like three weeks sooner.'

'So do I,' said Diana penitently.

'How about Craig, by the way? Any progress there?'

To Naomi's surprise Diana blushed vividly. 'Actually, yes. He took me out to dinner last night. That's why I wasn't around when you got back.'

Naomi's smile was bitter. 'Nice to know my sacrifice wasn't in vain.'

'Was it such a sacrifice, then?' said Diana swiftly.

'If you mean did I feel like a burnt offering by the time I left, yes!' Naomi pushed her sister towards the door. 'Now let me get to bed before Clare comes home and keeps me up half the night!'

Diana paused on the landing. 'Did Bran Llewellyn pay up, by the way?'

'On the nail. I received a cheque only today, via Diadem.'

The cheque, for twice the sum originally agreed, had been sent with a card inscribed 'Bran Llewellyn' in bold black typeface. On the back of the card, in what Naomi took to be Tal's handwriting, were the words, 'Enclosed your thirty pieces of silver'.

CHAPTER TEN

SUMMER came early that year. By the end of May London was sweltering in an early heatwave, ablaze with chestnut trees in blossom, and the scent of lilac was heavy in the quiet tree-lined road where Naomi shared an attic flat with Clare. When the sun shone Naomi learned to avoid Hyde Park, where she normally took her picnic lunch, unable to bear the sight of couples walking hand in hand, or lying entangled on the grass. She took to eating her chainstore sandwich at the desk in the little office in the basement, and assured herself that someday she'd get over Bran Llewellyn, just as she'd got over Greg. In theory it ought to be easier this time. She'd spent a whole year of her life with Greg, while all she'd been allowed with Bran were eighteen brief, unforgettable days in Wales.

'Naomi,' said Rupert one day, 'far be it from me to intrude on your private life, but Laura and I feel there's something wrong. That foxy little face of yours is growing thinner by the day. You're all eyes and bones, you know. Can we help?'

'I'm afraid not.' Naomi smiled gratefully. 'But it's very sweet of you, Rupert. Sorry I'm such a misery lately.'

'Man trouble?'

'You could say that.'

'Find another chap, Naomi.' Rupert's eyes twinkled. 'Laura says we're all alike, so a replacement should be easy enough.'

Naomi smiled wryly. 'Not for this one. But don't worry, I'll get over it. Eventually.'

'Of course you will. And as part of your recovery programme I suggest you stop incarcerating yourself in here day after day and go to a couple of sales.'

'Anything you say.'

Rupert patted her hand. 'Good girl. Sotheby's this week, then, and Cardiff next Tuesday.'

Naomi made a face. 'Sotheby's, fine, but not Cardiff, please, Rupert.'

Rupert's eyebrows rose. 'Ah! Right. I'll do that one, you do Lewes.'

Naomi nodded gratefully. 'Anywhere.'

'Bar Cardiff!' Rupert raised a hand. 'And don't worry. Discreet, tactful fellow that I am, I shan't ask why.'

'Thank you, Rupert. What price do you want on these Bristol vases?'

One evening, three interminable weeks after her return from Wales, Naomi gave in to Diana's coaxing and met her after work for a meal in an Italian restaurant near Sinclair Antiques.

'You look terrible,' said Diana.

'It's the heat,' said Naomi shortly, and changed the subject. 'How are things with you and Craig?'

'Fine.' There was a pause while Diana applied herself to an artistic plate of monkfish salad. 'In fact,' she went on, 'he's asked me away for the weekend.'

'Dear me, things are hotting up!'

Diana sighed. 'We had everything arranged for next week, to go to a literary festival, but now Craig's doubtful he can make it.'

'Pity—can't you go away some other time?'

'Yes, of course. But I really fancied the literary festival. Craig booked for a couple of lectures.' Diana smiled persuasively. 'Look, why don't you come instead?'

Naomi shook her head regretfully. 'Can't afford it.'

'Of course you can. Craig's paid for the tickets, and I'll treat you to a room—come *on*. A break will do you good.'

Naomi thought about it. As an alternative to a weekend spent sweltering alone in a London heatwave it was certainly tempting. 'Who's giving the lectures?'

'A man by the name of Benedict Carver's doing one,' said Diana smugly. 'How does a talk on eighteenth-century ceramics grab you?'

Naomi's eyes brightened. 'Why didn't you say that before? In that case I will come. Where's the festival?'

'Somewhere near Hereford,' said Diana vaguely. 'Fancy some pudding?'

With something to look forward to for a change, Naomi's mood lightened a little during the following week. She gave in to Clare's persuasion and went out to the cinema for the first time since coming back, and even enjoyed the film. The rawness of her agony over Bran began to lessen slightly, and when the shop was busy she even managed to go for minutes at a time without thinking of him, something which had been totally beyond her up to now. Every day since her flight from Wales she'd picked up the phone to apologise, longing to hear his voice, but her courage had failed her every time and she'd replaced the receiver without dialling, afraid he'd refuse to speak to her. And letters of apology were out of the question. Naomi had no intention of baring her soul for someone else, even Megan, to relay second-hand to Bran.

By the time Diana collected her early the following Saturday morning Naomi felt better than at any time since her return from Gwal-y-Ddraig. Diana's smart new Cabriolet ate the miles very comfortably as they bowled along the M4 towards their goal in the early morning sunshine, and for the first time in weeks

Naomi felt her spirits lift. Diana was a careful, smooth driver, and after a while Naomi grew drowsy, her run of wakeful nights taking their toll as she slid lower in the seat and gave way to the sleep her system craved.

When Naomi woke she found herself staring down at the wide waters of a familiar estuary as the car crossed the Severn Bridge. 'Hold on—what on earth are we doing here, Diana?' she demanded, sitting bolt upright.

'Craig planned the route for me,' said her sister as she turned off the bridge and made for Chepstow. 'He said this is the prettiest way.'

'And the longest,' retorted Naomi, her stomach churning at the discovery that she was in Wales again, breathing the same air as Bran Llewellyn. 'Surely this isn't the easiest way to Hereford?'

'Search me,' said Diana casually. 'Anyway the place we're heading for is quite a few miles from Hereford.'

'Diana,' said Naomi sharply. 'Where exactly *are* we heading for?'

'Hay-on-Wye, darling. Where all the bookshops are. You'll love it.'

Naomi gazed at her sister in horror. 'But Di, that's in Wales. Hay's not far from Llanthony! I'd never have stirred from London if I'd known.'

'That's why I didn't tell you,' said Diana, unrepentant. 'Now keep quiet while I look for signs. Apparently we don't go into Chepstow itself. We make for the racecourse roundabout where Craig says I take a left turning for Itton and Devauden, and keep straight on until I see a sign for Llansoy and Raglan. Now you're awake, do some navigating.'

Naomi subsided in her seat, simmering, but after a while her common sense reasserted itself. Hay was far enough from Llanthony to make an accidental meeting with Bran one chance in a million. And with his present handicap a town crowded with culture-seekers was the last place he was likely to visit, even with the faithful Tal in attendance. She forced her mind away from Bran, concentrating hard on the scenery instead as they drove along a quiet road edged in some places with walls, but mainly with hedgerows and green, hilly fields. At last she spotted the roadsign they were looking for and directed Diana to take a left turning for Llansoy, both girls exclaiming in unison at the beauty of the Vale of Usk spread out in panorama below as the narrow road swooped downward on its steep scenic way to Raglan and the bypass to Abergavenny. Naomi felt a sharp pang of pain as they sped along the faster, familiar road, but ignored it sternly as she pointed out the Sugar Loaf to Diana, making no mention of the fact that Bran's home was just beyond the mountains looming closer with every mile. Once Abergavenny was behind them she felt better. There were no reminders of Bran Llewellyn on the route which led past Crickhowell and on to Talgarth and Hay. Not that she needed any, thought Naomi bleakly. He was with her constantly, wherever she went.

They arrived in Hay-on-Wye in time for much needed coffee before a browse round the famous bookshops lining the streets of the town. Hay, they discovered, was not only a paradise for bibliophiles, but a delightful place of terraced stone cottages and steep streets, a covered marketplace and a cinema now crammed with books for sale instead of showing films.

'What time's the first lecture?' asked Naomi.

'Not until three. We'll have loads of time to find the chapel where your ceramics man is talking, so we'll have an early lunch,' said Diana.

'Fine. In the meantime let's go into that shop over

there. Fancy going halves on an antique map for Dad's birthday?'

Over lunch in the garden of a busy little café Naomi and Diana pored over a guide book which informed them that to the Normans Hay had been the gate to Mid-Wales.

'All that past blood and turbulence is hard to believe now,' said Naomi, shaking her head. 'It says here that nowadays the main excitements are the sheep sales and the literary festival.'

'Eat some of that salad,' ordered Diana.

'Not hungry.' Naomi glanced at her sister's plate. 'You haven't eaten much either — in fact you're very fidgety today.'

'Hay fever, I think,' said Diana, looking flushed, 'must be all the green fields everywhere. Come on, let's make a move. If the chapel's small you'd better be early to get a front seat.'

'Frankly I'm surprised Craig was interested in a ceramics lecture,' said Naomi as they strolled through the crowded town. 'Not his cup of tea, surely?'

Diana looked sheepish. 'Actually he booked that once he knew you were going. His interest was in the lecture by the BBC foreign news reporter in the main auditorium tonight.'

Naomi grinned. 'Yours too, no doubt! Does this mean you'd rather go back to the bookshops than listen to Benedict Carver?'

'Would you mind very much?' Diana smiled guiltily. 'I know you're riveted by bits of ancient china, but frankly they leave me cold.'

Naomi laughed, assuring her sister she'd enjoy the lecture far more on her own than with a companion bored to tears by the entire thing.

'I'll just see you inside, then,' said Diana, as they arrived at the chapel. 'Here's your ticket. I'll meet you back at the café at four-thirty.' She gave Naomi a hug. 'Take care.'

Assuring Diana she could hardly come to harm in a ceramics lecture delivered in a respectable Welsh chapel, Naomi settled herself in a place on the end of the front row. The building filled up rapidly, soon so warm that she was glad she'd given in to Diana on the subject of clothes. Instead of the inevitable jeans and jersey she was wearing a loose yellow T-shirt and a flowing green cotton skirt printed with lemons. Even so once the chapel was full it was so hot that she found it hard to breathe, and felt glad when Benedict Carver arrived dead on time to begin his lecture.

Naomi took notes as the ceramics expert began to talk, knowing Rupert would expect chapter and verse when she got back to work. She soon forgot the heat as the lecture progressed. Benedict Carver, she found, was not only an expert in his field, but such a witty, accomplished speaker that she was sorry when his talk was over and it was time to go looking for Diana.

As she moved towards the door in the rear of the crowd Naomi stooped to pick up her fallen notebook, and almost fell over as she was jostled. When a hand caught her by the elbow to haul her upright she looked up with a smile of thanks which changed to shock as she gazed up in disbelief into the intent face of Bran Llewellyn. Heat rushed into her cheeks, then receded with sickening speed, leaving her breathless and dizzy. Cold perspiration broke out on her forehead, the walls of the chapel spun round her and she crumpled into strong arms which shot out to catch her. When she came to she was sitting on one of the seats in the front row, supported against an all too familiar shoulder while a sympathetic woman held a glass of water for her to drink.

'Feeling better, dear?' enquired the woman with

sympathy. 'It was very hot in here today. Will you be all right now? I'm on duty at the auditorium soon.'

Naomi nodded dumbly, almost convinced she was hallucinating as she listened to Bran's assurances that he would take care of the invalid. When they were alone in the deserted chapel he slid a finger under Naomi's chin and forced her to look into the handsome, scarred face which haunted her dreams.

'So,' said Bran softly, his eyes bright with recognition, and something else less easy to define. 'We meet again. What cultural venues we choose for our accidental meetings, to be sure. First the opera, now an obscure lecture on eighteenth-century ceramics. But this time, I swear, I'm not the one who knocked you over.'

Naomi gazed at him in despair, realising that, while the miracle had happened and Bran could see again, he had no idea who she was other than the girl he'd bumped into in the bar of the New Theatre in Cardiff.

Belatedly she tried to free herself, but Bran kept a firm, impersonal arm round her waist. 'I shouldn't try to stand yet. Lean against me. You look distinctly seedy.'

Seedy! thought Naomi wildly. Frantic was more like it. This was a Catch-22 situation with a vengeance. If she opened her mouth to speak Bran would know who she was, but if she remained dumb he'd think she was a total idiot. Which, one way and another, wasn't far wrong.

'I can't get over my luck in running into you again,' said Bran, astonishing her. 'From the moment I saw you that night I've yearned to draw that face of yours. Your bone-structure had me itching for a pencil.' He smiled, his eyes dancing with a light which made Naomi dizzy again.

She gave him a dazed, speechless smile and scrambled to her feet, desperate to escape, but a long arm shot out to bar her way. 'No you don't, Cinderella,' he said sharply. 'You won't run away from me a second time —— ' He looked up with a wry, unsurprised smile as Diana came hurrying into the deserted chapel. 'Ah! The cavalry's arrived.'

'Hello,' said Diana, smiling guiltily.

'My fellow conspirator, I assume,' said Bran, holding out his hand. 'Good to meet you, Diana.'

Naomi looked wildly from one to another, dawning comprehension in her eyes. She heaved a deep, shaky breath. 'So. You knew who I was all the time, Bran Llewellyn. You were just playing with me,' she said bitterly.

Diana looked desperately uncomfortable. 'I sent him the snap Dad took of us on the lawn last year.'

'You sent Bran a photograph? How—why——?' Naomi's eyes filled with weak, angry tears and she bit hard on her lower lip.

Bran moved in closer, the eyes holding Naomi's as green and unreadable as bottle glass in the shadowed chapel. 'I contacted Diana to ask for a picture of you.'

Naomi eyed her sister in bitter reproach. 'Why didn't you *tell* me?'

'You'll never know the struggle I had to keep quiet about it!' Diana took her hand, squeezing it remorsefully. 'But Bran swore me to silence. He wanted to speak to you himself first. Don't be angry, love. At least it gave me the chance to tell him I was to blame for what happened.'

Naomi shook her head. 'Not entirely. You were the one who ordered me home the moment I got to Gwal-y-Ddraig, remember.'

'Is that true?' said Bran softly, his eyes gleaming.

Naomi's pallid face coloured painfully. 'Yes.'

'So why didn't you go?'

'I—I was committed to doing the job by that time. Once I found out—I mean once I——' She floundered at the look in his eyes.

'Discovered I was blind,' he finished for her, then smiled at her look of dismay. 'It's all right—Diana knows.'

Diana dropped Naomi's hand, frowning. 'Don't look like that—I won't rush straight back to the *Chronicle* with the news! Bran told me that in confidence.'

Naomi pulled herself together, and turned back to Bran. 'How long have you been able to see?'

'I was beginning to distinguish shapes before you ran away——'

'You *sent* me away!'

'Do you blame me?' he demanded.

She shook her head miserably. 'No.'

They stared at each other in tense silence, forgetting Diana, who was obliged to cough loudly at last to remind them she was still there.

'Look,' she said awkwardly, 'I imagine you two have a lot to talk about. In any case I'm meeting Craig at a hotel called the Swan at Hay soon so I'll go back there and wait for him.'

Naomi blinked in astonishment. 'Craig? But I thought——'

'Bran will explain,' said Diana hastily, and gave her sister a hug. 'Lord, you look peaky. Are you all right?'

'She'll be fine,' said Bran firmly. 'I'll take care of her.'

Diana gave him a long look. 'You'd better. See you later, then.'

By this time Naomi had given up asking questions. The whole day had taken on such an air of unreality that she wouldn't have been surprised to wake up in her bedroom in London and find she'd been dreaming.

'Are you feeling better?' asked Bran.

'I don't know how I feel,' she said, watching her sister hurry away. She turned to him shyly. 'I should have said so before—I'm very glad you can see again, Bran. Is your vision as good as before?'

'It is now.' He took her hand and led her to a chair. 'In the beginning it was grainy and indistinct, like an old black and white film. But bit by bit it grew clearer until the definition was back and I was seeing in Technicolor again.' He smiled quizzically. 'Though now you know I can see I'm surprised there's one question you haven't asked. Aren't you wondering why I haven't contacted you before?'

'I assumed you didn't want to,' she muttered, looking down at her tightly clasped hands.

Bran loosened them and took one small, clammy paw in his. 'Let's get one thing clear, Naomi Barry. When I told you to get out of my sight that day, I meant out of the way for a while until I'd recovered my temper, not out of my life! When I got back I went berserk when I found you'd taken off. I was so mad with you I made Tal post off that cheque—the one you sent straight back, incidentally. When Megan heard about it she wiped the floor with me!'

There was a long, tense silence.

'That was some time ago,' Naomi pointed out at last.

Bran let out a deep breath. 'I know. But I needed my eyes back in full working order before I could go racing off after you to London to drag you back by the hair. Then I realised I had no idea where you lived. I rang up Diadem and demanded your address, but all they could give me was the address of Sinclair Antiques, which you'd put on your application. Then it dawned on me that I had no idea what you looked like, either. It would have been bloody embarrassing to charge into a shop and grab the wrong girl!'

Naomi smiled a little. 'Bad for Rupert, too. Seeing me dragged by the hair through his shelves of priceless porcelain would have given him a heart attack.'

Bran grinned. 'True. Fortunately for him I abandoned this melodramatic scenario and contacted Diana via the *Chronicle* instead. I introduced myself, made one or two points crystal-clear, and then listened with great interest when she told me how worried she was about you.'

Colour flooded Naomi's face, then receded again, and Bran reached for her involuntarily.

She evaded his hands, shaking her head. 'I won't faint again. I'm merely suffering from embarrassment at having my private life made public. Diana's not usually so forthcoming to strangers.'

Bran raised a sardonic black eyebrow. 'I'm hardly a stranger where you're concerned, *cariad*. Nor do I ever intend to be. A point I had to make very clear before your sister would talk about you at all. Though it was my sob-story about the blindness that finally persuaded her to lure you here today.'

Naomi frowned. 'Why didn't you just ring me?'

'I wanted to meet you in person, not to talk to a voice.' He smiled wryly. 'But I needed a photograph to recognise you.'

Naomi stared at him woodenly. 'And so you saw my face at last.'

'Again, Naomi, not at last.' He smiled triumphantly. 'I'd seen your face before, remember. I could hardly believe my luck when I realised you were the girl at the opera.'

'Luck?' Naomi stared at him in disbelief, her heart thumping.

Bran grasped her by the shoulders, his eyes locked with hers. 'Yes. Luck. Good fortune, or whatever else you choose to call it. When I saw the photograph I offered up a prayer to the god of coincidence!'

She shook her head. 'There was no coincidence about it. From the moment I told Diana about bumping into you at the opera all she could think of was wangling an interview with you — the one you refused to every other member of the Press. Originally, heaven help me, I was supposed to buttonhole you at the Cardiff sale and trade on our chance meeting to get you to talk to her.'

'Only I didn't turn up.'

'Much to my relief.' Naomi pulled a face. 'Which was short-lived when Diana outlined the new game-plan she had waiting!'

They looked at each other in silence, Naomi still beset by so many emotions that she found it hard to sit still under the searching green gaze.

'I want you to sit for me, Naomi,' said Bran abruptly.

She swallowed, still finding it hard to believe that he wanted to paint her. 'Are you working again, then?' she hedged.

He nodded casually. 'Once the consultant gave the go-ahead I decided to get my hand in by finishing off Allegra's portrait.'

The news damped her down like a wet sponge. 'Ah, yes, Allegra. Did she come running back, just as I forecast?'

'She wanted to. Why? Are you jealous?'

'Certainly not!'

'Then why the hell ask?'

Naomi shrugged. 'Idle curiosity.'

Bran's eyes glittered coldly. 'I was quite happy to see her again, as it happens. Purely because, like the Greeks, she came bearing gifts. She was so keen to have the portrait I let her drive down to collect it, with Daddy's cheque in her hot little hand.'

'Was she pleased to know you can see again?' asked Naomi tonelessly.

Bran scowled at her. 'Yes. A bloody sight more than you seem to be, as a matter of fact.'

'That's not true!' said Naomi hotly. 'How can you say that? I know it's the most important thing in your life!'

He shook his head. 'One of the *two* most important things in my life.'

She waited, tense, and he smiled slowly.

'The other being the entry into my life of Naomi Barry, who turned out to be the girl at the opera — the girl whose bones made me itch to draw them. Don't look at me like that,' he added swiftly. 'I'm telling the exact truth. Afterwards, I had a clear view of you across the circle.'

Naomi stared at him, her mind going round in circles. 'I didn't see *you*.'

'I was at the back of a box, free to gaze at that face of yours as much as I liked, which was a damn sight more than my companion liked, believe me. She got very stroppy over it.'

'I can see why if it was Allegra. With a face like hers she must have found it hard to understand why you were fascinated by mine!'

Bran looked at her for a moment in silence. 'Naomi, why are you so paranoid about your looks? All right, so you're not conventionally pretty. Not in the way Allegra is, or your sister. But your bones are beautiful, and the way they contrast with that wide, full-lipped mouth of yours makes you a damn sight more interesting to draw than most women — ' He looked up suddenly, at the sound of voices. 'We'd better get out of here, or we'll be locked in for the night.'

He took the dark glasses from the top pocket of his jacket, then picked up a panama hat lying on a nearby chair.

'Disguise?' asked Naomi, as she slung her bag over her shoulder.

'No — protection. Now my sight is back I feel the urge to cherish it.'

They walked out into the bright afternoon, Naomi very conscious of the contrast they must present: Bran, tall and imposing in a fawn lightweight suit cut by some master Italian hand, the hat set at a rakish angle above the black lenses protecting his eyes, herself in her inexpensive chainstore clothes, her hair untidy after the rigours of the afternoon.

'I was to tell you,' said Bran, tucking her hand through his arm, 'that Craig Anthony will be escorting your sister to the lecture tonight, and then dining with her at the Swan at Hay, where they'll be staying overnight. Diana told me to say you're welcome to join them for all three if you prefer that to the alternative.'

Naomi looked up at him quizzically. 'Are *you* offering me the alternative?'

He gave her a glittering, assured smile. 'After all the cloak-and-dagger stuff with Diana to get you here in the first place, I should damn well hope so!'

'What do you have in mind?' she asked quietly, and Bran stopped dead in the middle of the pavement, obliging the flow of passers-by to part round them to get past. He looked down into her face for a long, searching moment, then began hauling her along at top speed.

'I'm taking you home,' he informed her, with a look which dared her to argue. 'The moment we've told Diana what's happened I'm driving you straight back to Gwal-y-Ddraig for as long as I can bully you into staying.'

For the rest of her life would do nicely, thought a dazed Naomi, hard put to it to keep up with the long, purposeful stride she'd always known must be characteristic of a Bran Llewellyn with twenty-twenty vision.

The meeting with Diana and Craig was convivial but brief, Bran so obviously impatient to have Naomi to himself that he would spare only the time it took for introductions and a few moments' conversation before spiriting her away.

'Did *you* tell Diana to have my overnight bag ready?' demanded Naomi, as Bran hurried her along to the car park.

He grinned. 'No. That was a dash of enterprise on her part.' He raised a challenging eyebrow as he unlocked the car. 'I could always drive you back later if you insist.'

Naomi slid into the passenger seat of a low-slung car in British racing green, impressed to recognise the Lotus Esprit Greg had always lusted after. 'Let's see how things go,' she murmured.

He smiled as he started the engine. 'Be warned. I'll do my damnedest to persuade you to stay.'

Naomi clenched her teeth against the wave of longing which swept through her, wrenching her mind from speculation about what form Bran's persuasion might take. Fortunately the route they were following was breathtaking enough to divert her attention very successfully, as he drove due south of Hay on a road which climbed gradually into the high country of the Black Mountains.

'They call this the Gospel Pass,' said Bran, as she gazed in awe at the panoramic views which appeared round every curve of the narrow, winding road. 'Legend has it that a daughter of Caractacus, the leader of the Siluries in the revolt against the Romans, invited St Peter and St Paul to preach the Gospel to her fellow countrymen here. The road's been given a better surface since those days,' he added with a grin, 'though I imagine the views are much the same.'

'It's magnificent,' she said breathlessly, 'but a tiny bit on the narrow side.'

'Plenty of passing places, *cariad*. Don't worry, I know it well. Soon we'll climb to about eighteen hundred feet as we leave the lower slopes of Hay Bluff, then we dive down into the Vale of Ewyas past Capel-y-ffin, and you'll be back on familiar territory.'

The journey through the Gospel Pass was an unforgettable experience for Naomi, not only for the scenic qualities of the route, but for the inexorable rise of anticipation overtaking her as their destination grew nearer with every mile. When the powerful green car purred up the drive to Gwal-y-Ddraig at last Naomi ran a comb through her hair and touched some lipstick to her mouth, to Bran's amusement.

Noting his grin, she shrugged, smiling. 'Just making myself tidy to meet Megan.'

Bran switched off the ignition and leaned forward to release Naomi's seatbelt. 'Sorry to disappoint you, Naomi—Megan and Tal are enjoying their annual holiday on the Gower coast. They go off to the Mumbles every year at this time without fail.'

The news affected Naomi like an electric shock as Bran leapt from the car and came to help her out.

'I suppose that means I'm cook again,' she said, trying hard for flippancy as she gazed in joyful recognition at the summer beauty of the gardens, where the liriodendron was now in full leaf as it towered in domination over the main lawn.

'We're a touch remote here to send out for a Chinese,' he answered in kind, and unlocked the front door. '*Croeso*, Naomi,' he said as he ushered her inside.

'What does that mean?' she asked, breathless suddenly as he closed the door behind him.

'Just welcome, Naomi,' he said simply, and put her grip on the floor. 'I'll leave this here — for the time being.'

Naomi flushed. 'Perhaps I could just go up to my room — I mean the guest room, and have a wash.'

Bran smiled and touched a hand to her cheek, sending another jolt of electricity through her. 'My house is yours, as they say in Spain. Go up and do whatever you want, then come down to the kitchen. From the look of you some food might be a good idea. What have you eaten today?'

'Just coffee, really,' she muttered.

His mouth tightened. 'I thought so — get a move on, then. I can't have you fainting on me again.'

'It's not a habit of mine,' she protested.

'Then why did you do it today?'

'It was the heat, I suppose. And the shock,' she added tartly.

'At seeing me?'

Naomi's long dark eyes met his without wavering. 'Yes, Bran. Shock at seeing you. I thought you'd never want to lay eyes on me again after what I did to you.'

He moved closer, until they were only inches apart. 'You were wrong, *cariad* — utterly, totally wrong,' he said softly, his eyes darkening until they were almost black. He breathed in deeply, then stood back, shaking his head. 'Don't be long, Naomi. Or I come and get you.'

She smiled in sudden elation, the light in her eyes transforming her face. 'Is that a promise?' But before he could react to the challenge she'd snatched up her bag and was racing upstairs.

Upstairs in the pretty, familiar room, Naomi took a hasty shower, suddenly crazily, madly happy now she was back in the lair of the dragon, where she belonged. She stopped short, staring at her face in the steamy bathroom mirror. Belonged? She nodded in reassurance to her reflection. From the look in Bran's eyes in the hall, just now, not to mention the lengths he'd gone to to get her here again, surely he felt the same?

Naomi brushed her hair until it gleamed, added a few touches of make-up to a face which already bore little relationship to the one she'd first confronted in her mirror that morning, then slid on the pink linen shift Diana had insisted on buying her to celebrate the new job. She smiled, remembering how she'd expected to wear it for a meal with Diana, never dreaming that her dinner companion would be Bran instead. Thoughts of dinner had her scurrying to find the pink linen pumps bought to wear with the dress, then she sprayed herself with perfume, threaded pearl drops through her ears and hurried from the room to find Bran halfway up the stairs coming to fetch her.

'Sorry I'm late,' she said breathlessly. 'I had a shower.'

'So did I.' His eyes travelled over her with a relish which brought the colour to her cheeks. 'You look better. Good enough to eat, in fact.'

'Talking of which, you'd better find me an apron. This dress is new,' she informed him as they made for the kitchen. 'Present from Diana.'

'You won't need an apron. Supper's ready,' said Bran smugly, and opened the kitchen door with a flourish to point at an impressive array of cold dishes on the table.

'I suppose you just threw all this together after you had your shower,' said Naomi, with the first genuine laugh she'd managed since the shock of meeting Bran again.

'Not exactly,' admitted Bran. 'I just took the dishes from the fridge, whipped off the covers and there you are. Cold buffet, kind courtesy of Megan. She only left this morning.'

And suddenly they were back to the rapport of the time spent alone before Bran knew about Diana's article. Naomi's appetite returned with it, her enthusiasm for salmon mousse and game pie equal to Bran's as he questioned her about the weeeks they'd spent apart.

'I was sure you'd ring me,' he said accusingly.

'I picked up the phone so many times I lost count, but I always chickened out, afraid you'd refuse to speak to me — especially after I received your cheque and accompanying note,' she added darkly.

'I was in such a rage I needed to lash out.' His mouth tightened. 'I got my just deserts when you sent it back with no note and no return address.'

Naomi met his eyes very squarely. 'I couldn't bear the thought of someone else reading my letter to you. And to put my address would have seemed like begging for a reply I knew I didn't deserve.'

They regarded each other in silence. 'These weeks without you have been purgatory,' said Bran at last. 'The only ray of light was my returning sight. When it was certain I'd see again I lost no time in planning a campaign to lure you, unsuspecting, back to Wales. First I had to persuade Megan and Tal to take their holiday a week early to coincide with the Hay Festival——'

'Why?' demanded Naomi.

Bran's eyes lit with a gleam which turned her bones to water. 'Because, my lovely, I wanted this place to myself when I finally brought you home again. Which is why I didn't come dashing after you to London the moment I could see. It was a gut reaction at first, I admit, but when I'd simmered down a bit and thought it over I realised it wasn't the ideal way to go about things.'

'Why not?' asked Naomi wistfully, thinking of the misery it would have saved her.

'Because I needed to see you alone, not with a flatmate in attendance, nor at Sinclair Antiques under the eyes of your boss and lord knows who else.'

'Oh.'

'So I contacted Diana instead and persuaded her to lure you to the literary festival, for which I'm deeply in her debt.' Bran smiled suddenly. 'I've thought of the perfect present to give her by way of appreciation.'

Naomi eyed him curiously. 'What do you have in mind?'

'I'll tell you later,' he said mysteriously. 'Right now I suggest we have some cheese, then we'll take our coffee to the studio. I might even get in a sketch or two of you before the light goes.'

Naomi's eyes narrowed. 'You mean you were actually serious about doing a portrait of me?'

He frowned impatiently. 'Of course I was serious! I've got the usual quota of faults, *cariad*, but insincerity isn't one of them.'

She smiled radiantly. 'Let's go now, then. I'll pass on the cheese. It keeps me awake.'

Bran took her hand and drew her to her feet, holding her lightly by the shoulders as he smiled down into her eyes. 'It just so happens I know an infallible cure for insomnia, *cariad*.'

'Do you, now!' she said breathlessly, wriggling free. 'I'll clear away. Do you know how to make coffee?'

'Not a clue,' he said shamelessly, and perched on

the table, one leg swinging as he watched her put the kitchen to rights. 'Let's have champagne instead.'

'Have we something to celebrate?' she asked, as they made for the studio.

'Oh, yes, *cariad*, we most definitely do,' said Bran very deliberately, in a tone which made Naomi's toes curl in the new pink shoes. He threw open the double doors and drew her into the room she'd last seen through a haze of agonised tears.

'I never thought I'd see this place again,' she said in a low voice, and went hurrying to look at the pictures on the walls as though greeting old friends, darting from one to another before coming to rest in front of Bran's self-portrait. She stood looking at it for so long that Bran called her name impatiently.

She turned to him, looking at him across the room with her heart in her eyes.

He caught his breath, and stretched out his arms. 'Come here. Now!'

Naomi went. She flew across the room like a homing bird, her face upturned to meet Bran's kiss as his arms closed about her. He picked her up and sat down with her on the familiar sofa, kissing her with a passion that reassured her more than any words could have done.

'What the hell did you mean by running off like that?' he said at last, panting. 'You knew I loved you, woman!'

Naomi's eyes opened wide on his. 'You never said so,' she whispered.

He scowled. 'Of course I did — well, perhaps not in so many words, but surely my actions spoke loudly enough?'

'A woman needs the words as well,' she informed him tartly.

Bran smiled down into her flushed, heavy-eyed face. 'Then listen well, my lovely, because in the future there may be one or two days when I forget to tell you, and I don't want you running off again. I've never loved any woman before in my entire life, unless you count my mother and Megan. I've enjoyed the company of a fair number of your sex, but never the same one for long. You're different. Small as you are, you feel like my other half, the missing piece that makes the puzzle of life complete.' He smiled with a light in his eyes which fairly blinded her. 'Now it's your turn. Tell me you love me.'

Naomi heaved a great shaky sigh. 'Of course I love you. These past weeks without you I've been so miserable I couldn't sleep, couldn't eat—why do you think I'm such a bag of bones?'

'Exquisite bones,' he said huskily, and began kissing her again. She responded fiercely, her body trembling under his urgent caresses until suddenly Bran stood up, holding her in his arms, his eyes burning into hers. 'I want you,' he said hoarsely.

For answer Naomi buried her face against him, kissing the strong, taut column of his throat, and Bran strode with her towards the spiral stair, and mounted it rapidly, breathing heavily by the time he set her on her feet beside his bed.

'Don't worry,' he panted, grinning. 'It's your proximity, not your weight, that's taken my breath away.'

Naomi's eyes danced wickedly. 'Good. I'd rather get up here under my own steam than find you'd run out of yours now we've finally got here!'

Bran's eyes filled with an unholy light. 'That's rash, fighting talk, *cariad*!'

'Only I don't want to fight,' she said, holding up her arms.

He pulled her hard against him. 'Tell me what you want, then.'

'I just want that wild delight your Dafydd ap Gwilym talked about — the one that ends in heart's possessing.'

'You've got my heart already, in the palm of your hand!' He tipped her face up to his. 'Give me yours in exchange and I'll take good care of it, I promise, in sickness and health till death us do part.'

'Is that what you want?' she whispered, her heart thudding against his.

'More than anything I've ever wanted before.' Bran kissed her gently, then less gently, the desire flooding through them both in such swift, overwhelming spate that there were no more words other than breathless endearments as his urgent, disrobing hands revealed the slender body he could now caress with his eyes as well as his clever, coaxing hands. And in the end there was no time, nor need, for the poet's 'long caressing' as their bodies merged in a union so perfectly attuned that it transcended the mere physical to create a fusion of heart, mind and soul.

'I'll always be grateful to Diana,' said Bran huskily, a long time later.

'For conspiring with you to get me to Wales again?'

'No — for her brilliant idea of getting you to come here in the first place.'

Naomi drew away, and propped herself up on one elbow to look down into his brilliant sea-green eyes. 'Bran, I love Diana, and I owe her gratitude for her love and support during a bad patch in my life. But I didn't come here just because she coaxed me to.'

Bran's eyes narrowed. 'Why, then?'

Naomi smiled mischievously. 'Let's put it this way. If Diana had wanted an article about anyone else I'd have flatly refused. But I'd already met you, remember. At the risk of inflating your ego, Bran Llewellyn, one look was all it took. I couldn't get you out of my mind.'

Bran shot upright to take her in his arms. 'You mean —— ?'

'Exactly! After seeing you that night at the opera I couldn't resist the temptation of meeting you again even if the price was a spot of spying for Diana.'

He breathed in deeply as he looked down into her face. 'I never thought I'd have cause to be thankful for my accident, *cariad*, but if the blindness brought you to me it was worth those weeks of darkness.'

She clutched him to her in fierce appreciation of the greatest compliment he could have paid her. Bran returned the embrace with such fervour that they were quickly engulfed in another tide of delight as wild as anything the medieval poet had ever envisaged. Afterwards they slept in each other's arms, until Naomi stirred to the touch of Bran's fingers as they stroked her cheek.

'Wake up, sleepyhead,' he whispered. 'I want to ring Diana in Hay.'

Naomi shook with laughter against him. 'Darling— at this time of night?'

He chuckled. 'It's only just gone ten, *cariad*. We came to bed rather early.'

Naomi stretched, yawning, suddenly aware that it was still light. 'I still don't know why you want to ring Diana.'

'I thought we'd announce our forthcoming marriage.'

Naomi lay very still against him, her heart thudding at the mention of marriage. She breathed in deeply, then reached up to kiss Bran's smiling mouth. 'You're really going to trust Diana with the news? She's with Craig, remember, and they're both journalists.'

Bran hugged her, laughing. 'That's the whole point, my lovely. It's my present to her — my way of thanking

Diana for sending you to me in the first place. What better way to show my appreciation?'

'You mean you're going to give her the exclusive all the gossip columnists would murder for?'

Bran held her close, smiling smugly. 'Absolutely. I can just see it in the *Chronicle*. "Welsh Artist Marries Beautiful Ceramics Expert" ——'

Naomi giggled. 'I'm no expert.' She pulled a face. 'I'm not beautiful either.'

Bran cupped her face in his hands, his eyes suddenly serious. 'Never say that again — much less think it. Always remember that I see you with the eyes of love, *cariad*. You'll never be anything but beautiful to me.'

Naomi smiled, her eyes incandescent through a haze of happy tears. 'Then in that case nothing else in the world matters!'

Welcome to Europe

WALES — 'the land of song'

One thing of which Wales can boast with pride is its variety — bustling cities and resorts contrast with sleepy villages and charming, timeless sandy bays. The scenery too is wonderfully diverse — from mountains to rugged limestone cliffs, lovely estuaries and giant, rolling sand hills. Add to this a wealth of flora and fauna and you have the essential natural beauty that typifies Wales — so for those of you who enjoy the great outdoors there is no better place to 'get away from it all'. . .

THE ROMANTIC PAST

Palaeolithic man settled in Wales around 10,000 years ago, and at the **Paviland Cave** in Gower the skeleton of a young man of that period was found sitting upright with all his possessions around him.

The forerunners of the Welsh population were Neolithic men who came from Western France about 5,000 years ago and settled on the coast.

Wales has numerous legends and folk stories. *Na.
Gwrtheyrn* is the story of Rhys and Meinir, who
wanted to marry, but tradition dictated that the bride-
groom must find his bride. So Meinir, being mischiev-
ous, ran off into the wood and hid in a dead tree trunk,
where, tragically, she got stuck. She was never found
and her lover, Rhys, was heartbroken; Meinir's skeleton was found many years later. Eventually the lovers'
village declined — the old people died and others
moved away; however, one of the derelict houses has
since been renovated and is now a **Centre for Welsh
Learning** where residential courses are held!

Another famous legend is that of the **Lady of Llyn-y-
Fan-Fach**. One day, near the end of the twelfth
century, a young man was tending his cattle near a
lake called Llyn-y-Fan-Fach, when he saw a beautiful
woman sitting on the surface of the water. Riveted, he
offered her some bread, but she refused, claiming,
'Hard baked is thy bread!' and dived under the water.
Next day the besotted youth returned and, when the
Lady reappeared, offered her unbaked bread, which
she also refused — but with a smile this time, so that he
was encouraged to try again.

Consequently, the next day the youth returned to
the lake with an offering of slightly baked bread, which
the Lady duly accepted. She then agreed to marry
him, on conditon that they should live together only
until he inflicted upon her three blows without cause.
If he gave her three such blows she would leave him
forever.

However, no sooner had the agreement been
reached than the Lady disappeared — only to re-
emerge with another woman, the mirror-image of
herself, and a man, who revealed himself to be the
ladies' father. He told the youth that he would consent

ɔ the marriage if the youth correctly indicated which of the two ladies was his betrothed. When one put forward her foot the young man identified her as his love because he had noticed before the way she tied each of her sandals differently.

Subsequently the marriage took place and, with a generous dowry in the form of sheep, goats, cattle and horses, the couple lived happily and prosperously for many years at a farm called Esgair Llaethdy, and had three sons.

One day they were preparing to go to a christening when the husband asked his wife to fetch a horse from the field while he went back to the house to fetch her gloves. But when he came back he found that she hadn't done so — and slapped her on the shoulder to hurry her along. Thus he unwittingly struck his wife for the first time without cause.

The second strike without cause was occasioned by his wife bursting into tears, quite inappropriately, at a wedding. When he touched her shoulder and asked what was wrong she claimed he had struck her again.

Several years passed; the sons grew to be clever young men and their father was careful to avoid inadvertently striking his wife, since one more blow and she would leave him forever.

One day, however, at a funeral, the Lady of the Lake so shocked her husband by laughing during the service that he touched her, telling her to stop. The Lady immediately declared that the third blow had been struck, and left, taking with her all the livestock that had been her dowry, and disappearing with them into the lake.

No one knows what became of her devastated husband, but it is said that her sons often went to the lake, hoping to see their mother, and that one day she did appear to her eldest son. She told him his mission on earth was to help mankind through curing them of disease, and gave him prescriptions and instructions to help him in his task. Her parting words to him were that if he and his brothers took heed of her instructions they would become the most skilful physicians in the country for years to come.

Welsh folk culture still thrives in the form of dancing, clogging and folk songs, which tend to be about lost or unrequited love.

The traditional women's costume, derived from peasants' clothing, is made from Welsh flannel and consists of a wool *betgwn* (bedgown) and wool skirt, with a long apron to protect the skirt while working. A hat called a Beaver is also worn.

Famous Welsh people include the poet **Dylan Thomas**, actors **Anthony Hopkins** and **Richard Burton**, singers **Tom Jones** and **Shirley Bassey**, and politician **David Lloyd George**.

THE ROMANTIC PRESENT — pastimes for lovers. . .

Where places to visit are concerned, Wales has so much to offer that we can only give you a taste of what to expect, and, for the benefit of those of you who have yet to go there, will concentrate on its two major towns, Cardiff and Swansea, and the surrounding countryside.

When you arrive in **Cardiff**, the capital of Wales, a good place to begin sightseeing is the **castle**, built in medieval times on the site of a Roman fort. The buildings were extensively revamped in the nineteenth century and the interior of the castle is now very impressive. The 150-ft clock-tower is a wonderful sight, with its pyramidal roof and coloured statues depicting the planets, and all around expect to see stained glass, rich carving, tiled floors and painted walls. Also worth seeing are the **Arab Room**, with its gold-leaf ceiling, the library, with its carved bookcases, and the **Summer Smoking Room**, located at the top of the clock-tower.

From the castle, take a short walk to **St John's**, Cardiff's sole surviving medieval church. Its tower, added in 1473, has a lovely pinnacled parapet; the rest of the church is mostly mid-fifteenth century, but underwent extensive rebuilding in the nineteenth century.

Next you might like to make your way to the **City Hall** — an impressive building with a clock-tower and superb marble hall in which statues of Welsh heroes are displayed — and then on to the **National Museum of Wales**, whose exhibits include a famous collection of French Impressionist and Post-Impressionist paintings, and Welsh views, as well as an impressive industrial section which has a full-scale reproduction of part of a coal-mine.

Just inland from Cardiff there are also many interesting sights. **Tinkinswood Burial Chamber** is one of the largest prehistoric tombs in Britain, dating from between 2000 and 4000 BC, and seven miles north of Cardiff you'll find **Caerphilly Castle**, Wales's largest castle, and second in Britain only to Windsor. It lies partly on the site of a Roman fort and was built in the thirteenth century — the leaning tower over the moat is the result of an unsuccessful attempt by Cromwell's troops to blow up the castle during the Civil War.

And not to be missed is the **Welsh Folk Museum** at St Fagan's, a charming little village to the west of Cardiff. Here, in the grounds of a carefully restored Norman castle, cottages, farms, shops, early chapels, a tannery, and even a working woollen mill have been painstakingly reconstructed to provide an accurate picture of the architecture and social life of Wales.

And now to **Swansea**. This town dates back to the Normans, but the ruins of what is known as **Swansea Castle** are in fact the remains of a fourteenth-century manor house. Not far from the town centre you can visit the **Royal Institution of South Wales**, which has interesting collections of archaeological, geological and historical exhibits, and the **Glynn Vivian Art Gallery**, with its paintings, sculptures and collections of glass, clocks, watches and Swansea and Nantgarw porcelain and pottery.

Since you are bound to want a souvenir of your visit to take home with you, Swansea is the ideal place to make your purchases. At the **Maritime and Industrial Museum**, located at the marina, there is a working woollen mill which produces high quality **woollen goods** made from the fleece of Welsh sheep and dyed in the traditional way; so here is where you can treat yourself to a lovely jumper to snuggle up in if the weather turns cold!

Alternatively, and perhaps more appropriately if you are holidaying with your lover, the **Welsh Lovespoon** is a popular souvenir. These were traditionally carved by a man for his betrothed as a sign of love. They can be very elaborate and have various symbols carved into them — for example, balls carved into the handle represent the number of children the woman can expect to have; a chain represents the chain of love; a key represents the key to the heart, to name but a few.

No visit to South Wales would be complete without a trip to the lovely village of **Mumbles** — the gateway to the beautiful Gower peninsula — and, for those of you seeking a different atmosphere from that of the cities, this is the place to head for. After all the sightseeing and shopping, the fresh sea air here will surely be invigorating and reviving! The peninsula is carved out of a plateau of limestone, with tall cliffs and pretty little bays complete with long stretches of sandy beach. A leisurely stroll with your lover along the cliff path will be one of the most romantic and memorable experiences of your holiday — imagine the glorious views, the sounds of the sea and the birds, the wind in your hair. . . Depending on how energetic you're feeling, you might reach the picturesque **Three Cliffs Bay**, where there is an attractive sandy beach — an ideal spot for a romantic paddle in the sea.

As far as eating and nightlife is concerned, there are several pubs and restaurants in Mumbles, but if you head back to Swansea you'll be spoilt for choice there too. The area is famous for its seafood, so why not try cockles, mussels or even a shark steak? *Laverbread* is also a speciality — made from seaweed and eaten fried with bacon. But if you fancy a hearty meal, you might like to sample the traditional *cawl* — Welsh broth made with lamb or mutton and vegetables — followed by roast honeyed lamb with cider and rosemary. Also, while you're in Wales, be sure to try *bara brith* — speckled bread — and the delicious *piceary maen* — Welsh cakes, cooked on a flat ironstone griddle.

If you fancy dancing the night away after your evening meal, Swansea has numerous clubs and discos, but for a more relaxed evening you might like to attend a classical music performance at the **Brangwyn Hall** — the setting for the highly acclaimed **Swansea Music Festival**, held every year in October. Alternatively, why not combine eating with entertainment at a **traditional Welsh evening**? These are held both in Swansea and at Cardiff Castle, and you can have an extremely enjoyable time eating traditional Welsh food while listening to Welsh folk songs and watching folk dancing and clogging, with the performers wearing traditional Welsh costume.

DID YOU KNOW THAT. . .?

* Wales is one of six Celtic areas, the others being Brittany, Cornwall, Ireland, Scotland and the Isle of Man.

* the Welsh language is closest to **Breton**, and onion sellers from Brittany still come to Wales to sell, being able to communicate quite easily with Welsh-speaking people.

* in the county of **Powys**, on the Borders, there are more sheep than humans!

* the **goldmines** of North Wales provide the Royals with gold.

* every summer the **National Eisteddfod** takes place — a huge cultural festival of concerts and competitions in music, poetry, drama, et cetera.

* the way to say 'I love you' in Welsh is '**Rwyn dy garu di**'.

**LOOK OUT FOR TWO TITLES EVERY
MONTH IN OUR SERIES OF
EUROPEAN ROMANCES:**

NO PROMISE OF LOVE: Lilian Peake (Switzerland)
Love-affairs by the dozen, but wedded bliss? Not for
wealthy Rolf Felder. So was his engagement to Abigail
merely a matter of convenience?

LOVE'S LABYRINTH: Jessica Hart (Crete)
Lefteris Markakis was arrogant, but undeniably attractive. The trouble was, he clearly despised English
girls—and Courtney had walked right into the middle
of his vendetta!

IN NAME ONLY: Diana Hamilton (Spain)
Javier Canpuzano had no doubt that Cathy was a bad
mother to little Johnny. What he *didn't* know was that
Cathy wasn't the child's mother at all. . .

MASTER OF DESTINY: Sally Heywood (Corfu)
Shelley had never forgotten Christos and their idyllic
summer in Corfu. Then love had turned to hate. . .
But now she was back, and Christos wanted his
revenge. . .

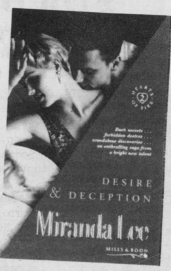
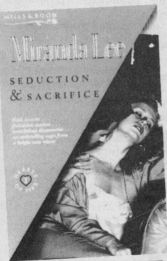

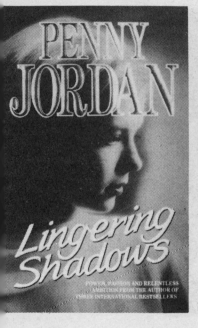

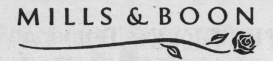

MILLS & BOON

Forthcoming Titles

DUET
Available in April

The Betty Neels Duet   **A SUITABLE MATCH**
THE MOST MARVELLOUS SUMMER

The Emma Darcy Duet   **PATTERN OF DECEIT**
BRIDE OF DIAMONDS

FAVOURITES
Available in April

NOT WITHOUT LOVE Roberta Leigh
NIGHT OF ERROR Kay Thorpe

LOVE ON CALL
Available in April

VET IN A QUANDARY Mary Bowring
NO SHADOW OF DOUBT Abigail Gordon
PRIORITY CARE Mary Hawkins
TO LOVE AGAIN Laura MacDonald

Available from W.H. Smith, John Menzies, Volume One,
Forbuoys, Martins, Tesco, Asda, Safeway and other paperback
stockists.

Also available from Mills & Boon Reader Service,
Freepost, P.O. Box 236, Croydon, Surrey CR9 9EL.

Readers in South Africa - write to:
Book Services International Ltd, P.O. Box 41654,
Craighall, Transvaal 2024.

Next Month's Romances

Each month you can choose from a wide variety of romance with Mills & Boon. Below are the new titles to look out for next month, why not ask either Mills & Boon Reader Service or your Newsagent to reserve you a copy of the titles you want to buy – just tick the titles you would like and either post to Reader Service or take it to any Newsagent and ask them to order your books.

Please save me the following titles:	Please tick	✓
AN UNSUITABLE WIFE	Lindsay Armstrong	
A VENGEFUL PASSION	Lynne Graham	
FRENCH LEAVE	Penny Jordan	
PASSIONATE SCANDAL	Michelle Reid	
LOVE'S PRISONER	Elizabeth Oldfield	
NO PROMISE OF LOVE	Lilian Peake	
DARK MIRROR	Daphne Clair	
ONE MAN, ONE LOVE	Natalie Fox	
LOVE'S LABYRINTH	Jessica Hart	
STRAW ON THE WIND	Elizabeth Power	
THE WINTER KING	Amanda Carpenter	
ADAM'S ANGEL	Lee Wilkinson	
RAINBOW ROUND THE MOON	Stephanie Wyatt	
DEAR ENEMY	Alison York	
LORD OF THE GLEN	Frances Lloyd	
OLD SCHOOL TIES	Leigh Michaels	

If you would like to order these books in addition to your regular subscription from Mills & Boon Reader Service please send £1.90 per title to: Mills & Boon Reader Service, Freepost, P.O. Box 236, Croydon, Surrey, CR9 9EL, quote your Subscriber No:.................................... (If applicable) and complete the name and address details below. Alternatively, these books are available from many local Newsagents including W H Smith, J Menzies, Martins and other paperback stockists from 8 April 1994.

Name:...

Address:...

....Post Code:...........................

To Retailer: If you would like to stock M&B books please contact your regular book/magazine wholesaler for details.

You may be mailed with offers from other reputable companies as a result of this application. If you would rather not take advantage of these opportunities please tick box ☐